ONE BAD WEEK

A
JONATHAN CROWLEY
CHRONICLE

JAMES A. MOORE

ISBN 978-1-63789-298-5
Macabre Ink is an imprint of Crossroad Press Publishing

For information address Crossroad Press at 141 Brayden Dr., Hertford, NC 27944
www.crossroadpress.com

First Crossroad Press Edition - 2025

Dedicated to Tessa Seppala, who makes me smile.

With Special Thanks to John McIlveen and Dan Brereton for reasons they already know.

Contents

Back to Serenity

October 31st

"Are you sure you're gonna be okay?" Dave shook his head and smiled. Her voice was soft and worried. Soft because she was at her boyfriend's place and he was probably sleeping. Worried because her baby brother was on his own on Halloween and she knew she should be at home.

"Amber, I'm not twelve." He tried to keep the exasperation out of his voice.

"I never said you were, I just don't like the idea of you being there all by yourself, or worse, having your friends over unsupervised."

"Well, no one said you had to stay in town with Barry."

There was a long pause. "Well, we're not hanging out at the farm so your pervo friends can try to sneak a peek."

"It's not all of them. These days it's just Tony. Okay, and Matt. But they're mostly harmless."

"It's the 'mostly' part that worries me, Dave."

"It's all good. No one's going anywhere. We're gonna watch a couple of crappy horror movies and get drunk."

"You aren't supposed to tell me that last part."

"Like it ever stopped you, being underage."

"Not the point."

"Yeah, yeah. I know. But it's all good. Have fun in town."

"All right. But you know where to reach me if you need me."

"Talk to you tomorrow. Or sooner if I have to."

"I love you, Dave." Ever since their family had been killed, Amber made it a point to tell him she loved him at least once a day.

"I love you too. Go. Have fun." Ever since she'd started saying it, he always returned the favor. It was part of how she coped, he supposed.

Halloween was in the air. The clouds that managed to hang around cut swaths through the sunlight and the cold winds whistled shrilly past headstones, and moaned through the trees. Leaves damned across the ground, surged like waves down lonesome, narrow streets and collected themselves at the corners of wooden fences throughout the area.

At the local Starbucks, yes, there was now a Starbucks in town; the flavor of the season was pumpkin spice.

There'd been a time when Dave Pageant would have cared, but those days were long past. At twelve years old his world was changed completely by the sort of things that Halloween celebrated and though he knew the season had nothing to do with his altered worldview, his joy of the macabre had been eliminated all of five years earlier.

Almost eighteen and most people who'd only known him when he was younger would have barely recognized him. He was taller now, obviously, but where he'd always been soft and had a round face, these days Dave was solid muscle and his features had hardened and become angular. These days he was no longer a boy. He was a young man and he shouldered the responsibilities that came with that title as easily as he'd always carried his chores on the farm.

Serenity Falls had been murdered by ghosts, demons and, worst of all, clowns. Dave watched it happen, saw his family slaughtered by the damned things. To say it left a mark on him was something of an understatement.

Clowns. That was what this all came down to. Some people had practically gone into mourning when the Ringling Brothers and Barnum & Bailey Circus failed. Dave had celebrated by knocking back a six-pack of tall boys. He would have done more, but even then he'd been preparing for this night.

Halloween, when the veil between the worlds is the thinnest.

For the last half a decade clowns had become Dave's obsession. He still went to school, he still did his homework and took care of the farm as best he could, but at the end of it all, he went back to studying the clowns.

It was creepy how many of the damned things there were in the world and how many seemed to frequent the world after their deaths. While he studied clowns in general, it was the tales of dead or undead clowns that got his full attention.

A lot of the claims about dead clowns led back to the same description, too. Dark blue hair, long and curly, a white face, blue triangles above and below the eyes. Blood red lips in a painted smile. Often found in street clothes and often reported at the locations of vicious murders.

There was little more than that to go on. No actual pictures. Just descriptions. Dave wasn't satisfied with that. He knew a clown that matched that basic physical profile, and he wanted to know if that particular harlequin was still alive.

Rufo the clown. The very creature that had murdered his family. Just thinking about him made the muscles in Dave's body want to lock up. Made his heart beat faster. Made the adrenaline start moving into his system. Was it a psychosis? Probably. But he was okay with that. Whatever helped get him through this night.

Natalie came into his office and tapped the sheaf of loose papers he had on the edge of the old roll top desk his grandfather had used for years. He doubted that damned thing had been moved in four generations at the old farmhouse. Why move it when it was already in the perfect spot?

He looked at Natalie and forced a smile. She was beautiful with her short dark hair, her brown eyes and her long, lean body. The glasses she wore only emphasized the shape of her face instead of obscuring her eyes. The outfit was a bit different, but she was dressed as a witch for Halloween. Some people still liked the holiday and he was not the sort to judge.

Besides, Natalie and the rest were here for him, and that was the part that mattered the most.

"You all ready with your notes and stuff?"

Dave looked away from her and back to the handwritten collection of markings and notes. Most of it was on his computer, but a few pieces would have to be transcribed to the laptop later. He wanted a record of his actions. He thought someday he might even write a book about what occurred, if anything, when he was finished.

Dave managed a smile for her. It felt wrong on his face. "Ready as I'm going to get."

He reached out and collected the top ten pages from the collected papers. They were still in order and he needed to keep it that way.

"Let's get to this. I want it done and over with."

Natalie smiled a bit nervously. She could still enjoy the whole concept of Halloween as long as it was make believe, but this? This was a different sort of thing entirely. This was, maybe, something real and dangerous.

Neither of them knew if anything would happen.

They would find out together.

November 1st

Tony Murphy was as drunk as he'd ever been and that was saying a lot. Both of his parents liked to drink and he never had a problem sharing their habits, especially after they went to bed.

At nineteen year of age he was still a senior in high school, but he was actually working on graduating this time around. He was limiting his drinking to the weekends and not finishing off whatever the flavor of the night was at home. It wasn't easy, because the spirits called to him.

He chuckled at that thought. "Spirits." He snorted a few small gasps of laughter and looked at the bottle of spiced rum currently perched between his tennis shoes. There were still a couple of sips worth and he intended to savor them.

Everyone else had gone inside and called it a night. It was after four in the morning, so that wasn't very surprising.

The trees around the Pageant farm were barren and looked like long, stretched out shadows of a hundred dancing skeletons to him. That might have been the booze or it might have been the holiday. In any event it was pleasantly creepy. The leaves slipped along with a cold wind and sighed and hissed as they found new places to be. The sky was clear enough, and the moon bright enough, that Tony decided to stay right where he was and enjoy the atmosphere, even if the air was cooler than he really wanted.

He changed his mind when he heard whistling coming his way.

It was a jaunty little tune, as his old man liked to say. Softly whistled through teeth and lips alike. The sounds weren't unpleasant, but something about hearing them in the absolute dead of night, after what they'd been doing earlier, made his skin want to slip away and hide.

The sound of heels tapping on the road was unsettling. A hard tak, tak, tak of boots moving down the paved access road to the farm chilled him even more. He knew that particular cadence though he couldn't have told you where he knew it from.

Tak, tak, tak. No kind of hurry. No sort of fretting, just a continuous sound that shouldn't have creeped him out as badly as it did.

Seeing the silhouette on the road didn't help. It was tall and lean and heading toward Serenity Falls. Was it human? Of course. Tony wasn't even sure why that thought popped into his head. Of course it was human! What else would it be?

Still, his pulse was too fast, and he was having trouble breathing properly, and he felt a sudden, powerful need to get up and be somewhere else, Oh, and to pee. His bladder was suddenly very unhappy with him.

"Well, is that Tony I see? Tony Murphy? When did you get all grown up?"

There it was. The voice was worse than the boot heels tapping. He knew that voice. Still couldn't place it to save his life, but he knew it. It was a voice that scared him as much as any boogieman ever had. It was a voice from when he was younger, not as quick to defend himself. It was a voice that had called out his name a thousand times and each time there was a teasing quality that was almost a guarantee of troubles to come.

"Marco? Is that you?" Marco Demillio. The kid most likely to give a kid a wedgie or a swirly, or an Indian sunburn. The terrorist who haunted the school yards throughout Serenity Falls until he vanished five years ago with the rest of the bastards who'd made Tony's early years a nightmare of torments.

He was sweating and his heart was hammering away, like it wanted out right damn now and needed to find a different body to occupy.

The head of the silhouette tilted. "Yep. That's right. It's me."

Tony shook his head. The shape was too tall for Marco. That was one of the reasons the guy was always such a prick, he was short and knew he'd never get taller. At least that was what Dave said and Dave was smart like nobody's business.

He almost told Marco he was too tall, but he thought better of it. Maybe he was wearing boots that gave him a few inches. Those things existed, right? Sure they did.

Tony squinted, trying to see Marco's face a bit better.

"Everybody's been saying you're dead, man."

"Nope. I'm right here, Tony. Just got a call telling me to come on back home, so I thought I should answer it, is all." Marco's voice sounded funny, like he was trying to hold back a laugh and barely succeeding. "Not really sure why," he frowned. "I really hate this town. But what can you do? Someone asks you to visit, seems rude not to at least pass through. I mean I can't *stay*. I have other things to do. Places to go. People to…see."

Tony shook his head, suddenly even more scared than he'd been before.

"Marco, I mean it. People said you died back when the tent showed up."

The lean figure stepped closer and Tony decided it was time to stand up, he didn't want to get caught sitting on his ass if Marco tried something.

"Tony, if I was dead we wouldn't be talking." That voice sounded so damned smarmy, like Marco was in on a joke that he knew Tony didn't understand and would never get.

"Well, maybe you should talk to the cops. I mean, they think you're dead. I heard something about the probate courts getting ready to say it officially."

"Tony, I'm surprised at you, I didn't even think you knew what a probate court was."

That was about it. The fear that had been gnawing at Tony's guts faded away quickly and he scowled. Alcohol sometimes made him angry. That was the problem with Marco. He was a bully, and an asshole, and he liked insulting people, but Tony wasn't the same kid he'd been five years ago. Back then he was always afraid of Marco. These days he'd learned a bit about defending himself and he wasn't going to take that shit off of the bastard.

"Know what your problem is, Marco? You're a prick. You're a stupid, ignorant asshole." The world was tilting a bit on its axis, but that was okay. Tony looked at Marco and figured he could take the bastard.

He looked up into the shadows where Marco's face was hiding and stared hard at what he thought was the right area for eyes. It was hard to tell through all the shadows, but he was willing to bet he was at least close.

"Know what your problem is, Tony?"

"No. What?"

"You think you're dealing with Marco." The hand that caught his wrist felt like it was all bones and hot, dry skin, like a mummified claw left out in the baking sun of a summer afternoon in Death Valley.

"Let go of me!" Tony tried to pull his hand away but that horrid cluster of spidery fingers clutched all the tighter.

"Marco wasn't all that good at getting away, either."

Tony swung his free hand in a hard arc, aiming to knock Marco's face off.

Marco leaned back and the wild fist soared right past where his face should have been.

"Tony, you have some strange friends. They invite me here and then leave you out as the welcome wagon."

"What are you talking about?" Tony cocked back his fist to try a second time, the man and the road before him tilting hard to the left as the alcohol in his system put a deep spin on his vision. He was pretty sure puking was going to happen soon, but first he had to kick Marcos's ass.

"I'm only here because your buddy Dave asked for me." The amusement in that voice was infuriating.

A flick of the wrist on Marco's part and Tony felt his own wrist explode into white-hot pain.

A second later he was doubled over and vomiting all over dirt and on his bottle of spiced rum. His arm was the only thing that didn't join him in his efforts to bend forward. The arm stayed where it was, held by Marco DeMillio's hard grip. Through the spins and the pain and the nausea, Marco held on.

"When did you take up drinking, Tony?" The voice was wrong. The bastard was laughing at him. "Didn't watching your parents drink their nights away teach you anything at all?"

Tony tried to stand up and the pain in his wrist shattered all efforts. He groaned and felt his knees go weak.

"So, listen, Tony. Nothing personal here, but I think Dave needs a reminder of why it's rude to call somebody so late at night. Back in my day? You never even considered calling someone after eight o'clock in the evening if it wasn't a serious emergency."

Tony looked down at the ground and studied the puddle of puke that covered his remaining rum. The thought of another drink was suddenly absolutely abhorrent.

"And you, Tony? You're no one's idea of an emergency. This is going to hurt, and it's going to hurt a lot, but try not to scream too much. We don't want to spoil the surprise, okay?"

He finally looked up and as he did Marco shifted enough that his face could be seen past the heavy, dark, curly hair around it.

The skin was too white. His lips had been painted a deep crimson and that red led into a smile that exaggerated the expression on Marco's face. When his real lips moved within that crescent grin it was unsettling.

"Gotta tell you, kid, I actually expected better from you. You always seemed like you were gonna make it, I mean even after I was done killing the town."

Marco's grip stayed strong and impossible to break, though Tony tried several times.

Despite what the man asked of him, Tony screamed as the tortures started in earnest. Long before they were done with, his screams had faded to whimpers.

When Dave opened his eyes the sun was glaring into them with a vengeance. He felt hung over, wrung out and left to dry in the noonday sun. All of which would have been fine and well deserved if he had actually had anything to drink the night before.

Everyone had stayed over. It was for their own good. He'd known the rituals would take a lot of energy, had expected that most everyone would be sore and stiff. What he had not expected was the pounding headache and the sudden allergy to bright lights.

"Ow." It was a small exclamation of his pain, but anything larger would have split his skull open.

Natalie rolled over on his bed and looked at him. There was a moment when he thought maybe they'd finally broken the rules and gone beyond an occasional kiss or handholding incident, but both he and she were still clothed.

Just as well. If they ever did hook up, he wanted to remember it.

"Did it work?" her voice was raspy with sleep. That only made her sound even more desirable.

Dave pushed himself into a sitting position and reached for his cigarettes. There were none there. He thought about it and once again resolved not to smoke any more. It wasn't worth the cost and he truly got no joy from the process.

"I don't know. I guess we'll have to find out." His own voice was rough and Dave reached for the bottle of water he usually found on the nightstand and frowned when he saw nothing there.

He sighed, shook his head and then stood up on legs that felt achy and weaker than they should have.

"Where you going?" Natalie's voice was playfully pouty. Not for the first time he wondered why they were together. They had very little in common that wasn't physical in nature and unlike the girls he'd grown up with, she was from a different area entirely. She'd moved to Serenity a little over a year after the circus fire and had only come into Dave's life accidentally.

She'd been out looking around the area for a place where she could keep her horse. The house where she lived was hardly large enough to allow the poor beast a decent area to run in.

When she'd knocked on the door and seen Dave she'd smiled. That was all it took for him to want to know her. Now, years later, her horse—Samson—still stayed at the Pageant Farm and Dave still charged her for the food and care he provided, but they were friends and sometimes he thought there was a chance that they would become more.

Most of the time he thought it was a pipe dream. They'd never done anything stronger than kiss and that had only happened on a couple of occasions. Damn near everyone thought they were together. Dave had no idea what to think, but Natalie always said they were just friends. That didn't bother him too much except for the occasions when she woke up in his bed.

According to the last will and testament of, well, everyone who had been murdered in the Pageant family, the land was to be divided between all of the children who wished to remain on the farm. The reality was a bit different. Dave lived on the farm and his two remaining siblings lived there as well, but the twins had moved on in many ways.

Amber and Suzette Pageant, the twins, had jobs in Serenity Falls proper. They had their own lives. Sometimes they even stayed at the apartments they had in town, like they had last night. Not because they had any problems with what Dave was trying to do, but because they knew they'd never be able to convince him not to do it and they didn't really like having other people over when they were trying to sleep. It had been cute when young Dave's friends had stumbled across their rooms when they were younger. It wasn't so cute anymore, and no matter how many times Dave told people to leave his sisters alone, they somehow managed to interact.

Some of his friends were assholes, and he knew it. But they served a purpose.

Dave stayed at the farm. He preferred it that way. He took online college courses, and he studied hard, and he took care of maintaining the farm and hiring the employees that helped out along the way. He'd been farming his entire life, ever since he was old enough for chores, which meant since he was eight.

Somehow he reached the kitchen and the coffeepot that waited there for him. He even managed to brew his much-needed black gold.

Ten minutes after finishing two mugs of the stuff he started feeling human again.

Not long after that point, the police arrived.

It wasn't the first time death had occurred at the Pageant farm, but it had been a while since the black carnival tent had risen from the ground and hundreds of locals had come to the farm seeking entertainment and received a death sentence instead.

They'd burned, assisted into the funeral pyre by none other than Rufo, the demented master of ceremonies at a carnival by, and for, the deceased. Dave had been there for part of it. Only part. He still bore the scars on his face from Rufo trying to carve his skin away. They paled when compared to the scars from having his entire family slaughtered, but they were still there, and not complete faded, despite plastic surgery and the years.

That was the problem, really. Dave couldn't move past what had happened.

The cops didn't care much. They weren't there to discuss the past. They wanted to understand what had happened to Tony Murphy.

Tony Murphy was a troublemaker from far back. He had a record of truancy problems and his adolescent rap sheet was the sort of thing that nearly guaranteed he'd be in trouble with the law in the future. Mind you, that had all stopped around seven months earlier, when he'd become friends with Dave. They started hanging around and the second time Tony ran away from a case of shoplifting—as if anyone in a town the size of Serenity Falls had to worry about identifying a criminal—Dave made it clear that he wasn't in the mood to play twenty questions with the police whenever Tony got himself in trouble. Tony decided he'd rather hang around with Dave than with the guys who kept encouraging his attempts at becoming a petty thief, from there things got less complicated.

The night before was a blur.

Dave remembered moving to where the bald spot on the ground was permanently burned into the earth of the farm. The exact spot where the Carnival of the Fantastic had risen from the soil was forever ruined for farming. It had been ever since the first carnival, when several of the locals had lit fires and killed the performers staying on the spot, back in the middle of the last century, and it was still the same situation decades later.

He remembered marking the vast circle in the soil, using salt and colored sand and chalk.

He remembered making his little offerings of the four elements for what was supposed to be a white magic incantation to summon the spirit of Rufo the Clown and then to bind that spirit if he could, the better to question the damned ghost, to torture the murderous wraith and then to banish said dead spirit to Hell if at all possible.

His intentions were not good, but they were pure in his eyes; he wanted to rid the world of a spirit that was corrupt and evil. He wanted to cleanse that spirit from existence and regain a bit of his own life in return. If he knew that ghost was bound and locked away from the world, then maybe, after five years, he could finally sleep again.

There were no guarantees, but he could hope. He could pray. He could try. That was what it all came down to. He had to try, because not knowing? Not trying to make certain the fucking ghost was finished once and for all was going to drive him bugshit crazy if he kept on the same path.

Stan Long had been like a brother to him when he was younger, had been his best friend for years on end. Stan died that miserable night five years ago, too. Had he been around he would have made sure that Dave took course corrections, that he stayed on the side of the sane. Stan could always do that for him, just as he could for his brother from another mother.

But Stan could not talk him out of anything. There was no ghost of his old friend that he could find. Stan was dead. Deceased. No longer among the living. There were a hundred ways to say the same thing, but they all came down to words and nothing else.

Stan's family had left town a long time ago. Even the memories of that family were faded into the past.

So instead Dave tried to work magic to get his point across. He wasn't sure if he'd failed or not, but one thing was absolutely certain: Some time during the night Tony's body had been nailed to the road at the very northernmost edge of the Pageant property. Roughly an hour ago, someone had found the body the hard way and wrecked the chassis of their car when they ran over the remains.

Victor Barnes, the largest man on the Serenity Falls police force, was the man who came and knocked on the front door and asked, again, if Dave knew anything about Tony's whereabouts. He was gentler than usual as he asked, and that alone left Dave with a frost pit where his stomach should have been.

The situation was made worse because the last time he'd seen Tony, that he could clearly recall, was when his friend was sitting across from him while he read the lines he needed to use for the summoning spell.

"Dave? You okay? I know he was your friend...." Vic's voice was as deep as his body was tall. The man was genuinely huge. His dark red hair was shot with silver these days, but otherwise he'd changed little since he came to Serenity Falls on his Harley and decided to stay. His eyes were kind and he was a good man, but not one that should ever be angered.

"I'm just. I don't know." Dave shrugged.

"When did you see him last, Dave?"

"We had a little bonfire here, last night. Nothing all that special. Tony was here, but we didn't get to talk much."

"Do you know who he was hanging around with?" Vic didn't ask if there had been drinking involved. That wasn't what this was all about. It was a murder investigation, pure and simple and that was his priority. Also, he knew good and well that Dave drank from time to time. So did damn near every kid at the high school, but Dave and his closest buds never got into any trouble. That was mostly because the drinking happened on the farm and stayed there.

"No, not really. I was kind of busy hanging with Natalie."

As he expected, Vic nodded at that answer, the constable was a good man, but he was also predictable. He expected Dave to try to get into Natalie's pants. That was what he, himself, likely would have been going for when he was younger. That's what Dave would have been doing on most nights, even if he were more passive about it.

But there was the ceremony to consider, and the rituals, and the ingredients, and what the fuck had happened to Tony? Dave looked toward the northern end of the property. He couldn't see the road. But he could imagine it. He could just make out the flashing lights from a couple of squad cars and maybe an ambulance.

"Who'd do that, Vic?" It was an honest question and one that slipped past his lips before he knew what was happening. "Who'd kill Tony? He was about the most harmless guy I knew."

The man shook his head and frowned. "Can't say, but I plan to find out." Vic shrugged his massive shoulders and looked down at Dave. He was reminded, again, exactly how big the man was. "You mind if I look around and check with anyone else hanging around?"

"Yeah. Do your stuff." Dave even held the door open for him. It was likely that most of his friends had made themselves as scarce as they could while he was talking with the man. Most of them were exactly the sort that tried to avoid making eye contact with cops. Speaking to them? Not if they could avoid it.

There were two other constables looking the place over. Neither of them had much to say to Dave, though both of them nodded their heads when they saw him looking. He waved a return hello and went about his business.

Vic came out fifteen minutes later. Natalie came out with him, but as Dave had expected the rest of the gang was already gone.

By the time Vic met up with him the ambulance was leaving, lights flashing but silent, and the other cops were clearing up their examination and heading back to Serenity Falls proper.

Autumn was upon them and the winds that blew across the emptied fields were kissed with the promise of winter.

Vic looked at his notes and sighed.

"I saw the papers next to your computer, Dave."

"And?"

Vic looked at him for a long while, his eyes trying for whatever was hidden inside of Dave's mind. "I don't know what you're up to, but I wish you'd let it go. You look at that sort of stuff too long and you might very well invite trouble back into our lives. The sort that no one here needs." The man was sincere and Dave knew it.

Dave nodded. The warnings were well meant but useless. "Just making sure I'm prepared if anything ever happens again, Vic."

Vic sighed again and closed his little notebook. He looked hard at Dave and Dave did his best not to flinch. Vic was a good man, but he could be a touch intimidating. "I've got a dollar that says you're lying to me. If I could bet against a minor, I might even suggest you pony up a dollar of your own. I find out you're up to anything, we're going to have words again, Dave. You get me?"

"I get you."

Words again. Again, because there was a little while after the clown was done when Dave lost it. He was a very intelligent young man and he'd actually tried summoning a few things that he shouldn't have. He'd failed in every summoning, but there had been a few unusual side effects to his attempts, not the least of which was disturbances at the local cemetery. He had no idea how Vic had guessed who the culprit was, but the man had come by the farm and taken the books he found on all subjects related to the supernatural. He had also called Jonathan Crowley out to look around.

Victor Barnes was a behemoth, he looked big enough to take on a bear and win, and he was well-trained in hand-to-hand combat, in addition to his skills with firearms. He was a marksman. Maybe not the top of his class, but capable of hitting a target if he set his mind to it. Before he'd come to the 'Falls he'd been in the army as an MP. He knew his shit and he was scary.

Next to Crowley he was not even a little disturbing as a possible enemy.

It was Crowley that eventually drove the evil out of town. It was Crowley that had taken out Rufo the Clown and had burned down the carnival. It was Crowley that had forced the dead away from the living and restored what was left of Serenity Falls to a semblance of normalcy.

Crowley seemed mild mannered enough, but once you got his attention, once he decided you needed to be punished, he got absolutely terrifying. Dave was a kid, so he let him off with a warning and a promise to make him suffer if he ever tried summoning anything again.

"I'm not up to anything, Vic. I just keep hearing rumors about a clown that sounds too familiar. I wanted to make sure he's not around."

"And I get that. Just. Just don't start something you can't finish, okay?"

Vic gave him a light cuff on the shoulder and started away.

"And Dave?"

"Yeah?"

"I'm sorry about your friend."

Dave nodded, even though he knew the man couldn't see it, and then he explained to Natalie what was going on.

She took it as poorly as he expected.

Serenity Falls is barely a speck on the map. Nestled in upstate New York the city's biggest claim to fame is the granite that comes from the area. It's high quality and abundant. And thanks to the Dunlow family the quarry is once again active. The town had been nearly dead when they came in and started working the area.

Despite the massive fire that killed over seven hundred people, the town of Serenity Falls was thriving. Had they offered the property up for sale, the Pageant clan would have made a very handsome sum, enough to leave them all incredibly comfortable for the rest of their lives. So far that was not an option, not for Dave or his older sisters, but it was a subject that came up from time to time.

Much like the subject of Dave's obsessions.

Victor Barnes loved the little town. He was rather fond of the Pageants' too. Dave was a good kid when he wasn't being stupid and his sisters, though far too young, were both lovely and liked to flirt with him. It was flattering and harmless.

He walked along the edge of their property and soon found what he was looking for. Railroad tracks. They'd long since been out of use and the last time anything of significance had traveled long them it had been a spectral train made real. When he wanted to have nightmares he remembered examining the train and the resulting hell that came to Serenity Falls back in the day.

He tried not to dwell too much.

What he was looking for was simple enough: he wanted to find a match for the metal spikes that had been rammed through the murder victim's body.

He found them easily enough, after only ten minutes of looking, railroad spikes and old ones by the looks of them. They were rusted and bent and with minimal effort he spotted several around the path that had once been used to convey property from one spot to another.

They were close enough for government work. While the railroad spikes were not the ones used to hammer a poor kid to the ground they were definitely neighbors.

Vic looked around the area and sighed. There were procedures to follow. He took a few photos of the spot and then called it in.

He'd wait for the forensics team to come back and look the area over.

In the meantime, he would consider whether or not he believed, even for a second, that Dave Pageant wasn't a part of the whole damned mess.

December 15th

Bill Kirby had lived in Serenity Falls for his entire life and since the age of sixteen he'd been working at Kirby's Rexall Drugs. It had belonged to his father before him and his father's father before that. Three generations of the family had owned and operated the place and the one thing that had stood true through all of that time was that loyalty was rewarded and theft was punished. There was a Wall of Shame clearly displayed on the wall facing the actual pharmacy. The words were penned in permanent marker, and the pictures were nailed in place and locked behind a Plexiglas security window. You did a crime against the place, your picture was taken and posted. No words were used, just the images. If anyone wanted to know what someone had done, they'd be told without hesitation.

The only way off that wall was to die. There had been one kid, Edward Pine, whose parents tried to sue to have the picture of their shoplifting, would-be molesting, son taken down after he was caught raiding the ladies' room. They'd tried. They'd failed. It came down to freedom of speech and since no accusations were posted, even if the pictures were, there was no violation of anyone's civil rights.

Even if there had been a violation, Bill wouldn't have given a good goddamn. It was his place. No one had to come in and shop there, but if they stole from him, or tried to, they got punished.

Bill's son would be taking over one day, but for now Hank was off in college, learning all about medicines that he had already studied under his father. For now, the Wall of Shame stayed where it was, though his pride and joy had already said he'd take the thing down some day. Until then the criminally disposed would stay up and anyone who asked would be told why they were posted there. Most of the people who'd been busted refused to show their faces again, and that was just fine with Bill.

So Bill was a bit surprised to see Marco DeMillio come waltzing into his store.

The bastard came in, a smirk on his face, looked right at Bill and winked. Then he moved further into the store, walking slowly down the aisles.

For a moment Bill couldn't move. He'd known Marco for as long as the little shit had been alive. Had seen him when he was young and innocent, had watched him grow darker, cockier, and finally become a thief and worse.

He surely didn't expect the twerp to show up in his place of business, especially since he'd been gone for over five years. The only thing he could give the boy credit for was having better taste in clothes. He was dressed in a nice suit under a trench coat to hold the cold at bay.

Marco looked right at him as he entered. And he smiled. Easy as you please, like he'd never done anything wrong in his life and he didn't deserve to be on the wall.

Bill looked at the wall of shame again, just to make sure. There was Marco's picture. He was scowling instead of grinning, but the old picture showed him after the cops had been called and he'd been busted with four cans of beer shoved into his pockets.

Bill nodded his head and reached for his cell phone. The police would probably be delighted to hear that the little bastard was still alive. There had been quite a fuss when he left with his friends and never showed his face again. Probably he had a list of things they'd want to talk to him about.

Bill moved toward his office in the very back left corner of the pharmacy, where people were not allowed, and listened to the phone ring against his ear, until he was rewarded with a masculine voice's response, "911, what's the nature of your emergency?"

"I wanted to report that I have found a missing person."

There was a momentary pause. "Can you state your name for the record, please?"

Bill smiled as he moved to the seat behind the old metal desk that had filled half of the small room for as long as he could remember. He sank into the heavy cushions and smiled. Three different cameras in three separate corners all filmed what was happening in his store. On them he could clearly see Marco moving along just as easy as you please, not a care in his little world.

Bill narrowed his eyes, moderately annoyed. "Johnny Upkins, you know good and well that this is Bill Kirby at the Rexall." It was a small town. Everyone knew everyone, whether or not they liked to admit it. "Marco DeMillio is walking around inside my store, easy as you like, and I believe I heard he was declared missing a few years back, so I wanted to report it."

Johnny sniffed. He was a good kid, but suffered mightily from the stick up his posterior, same as his mother before him.

Johnny sniffed a second time, because apparently once was not enough. "He was actually reported alive and well in Virginia last year. They found his fingerprints at a crime scene."

Bill nodded though the man could surely not see it. "Not at all surprising, given his background."

"I'll have someone sent along straight away, Mister Kirby, and thanks for the heads up."

"Only way to keep the town clean is to let the right people know when trash shows up." Bill chuckled a bit at that, amused by his own joke.

His eyes scanned over the monitors and he frowned. "Might need them to get here quickly. Looks like he might have left the building, but it was him and I'll testify that if I need to." There were places the cameras could not see, of course, but most of the store was there, even if the details got lost now and then. He could see Delilah at the front register, chewing her gum and looking at magazines instead of doing anything useful. She was a pretty enough little thing, but not exactly what one could call smart. He'd known that when he hired her. She was employed to ring people and to look good. That was all he cared about when it came to the girl. That, and she wasn't the sort to steal from the till. Not exactly creative enough to make use of her brains along those lines and not dumb enough to forget the camera aimed over her shoulder.

She looked up at the camera and adjusted the front of her work smock, baring just a touch more cleavage. Sometimes he thought the girl was flirting with him, but he wasn't foolish enough to consider acting on that notion. The girl was barely out of high school and his youngest kid was already in college. Looking was all he'd ever do, but he could enjoy the show with the best of them.

Johnny said something in his ear and took away the mild, but pleasant, fantasies Bill was having about his clerk.

"Come again, Johnny? You're breaking up a bit."

"I said Kyle Miller is on his way. According to our files Marco DeMillio should be considered armed and possibly dangerous, so you might be best staying away from him."

Bill considered the pistol he kept in his desk.

"Not to worry. I can handle myself, but thanks for the warning."

It had taken him a few years to get a carry and conceal license. New York was a bit strict about firearms. Just the same he had the weapon and he wasn't afraid to slip it into the shoulder holster under his white smock.

Damned if he'd ever let himself be afraid of some little sociopath with delusions of grandeur.

One last look at the monitors, to make sure that everything was in order, and Bill climbed out of his comfy chair and headed for the main store.

Marco was waiting just past the reach of the swinging door, a smile plastered on his face.

"Nice to see you again, Mister Kirby." Marco's blue eyes regarded him with merriment.

Blue? Aren't his eyes brown?

He considered the picture on the wall of shame and shook his head. His lips pulled down into a slight frown. Definitely brown, he'd have remembered eyes that startling on color.

"Marco. I thought you'd long since left town."

"I did." The smile was bright and pleasant, but it faded from his eyes as he looked at the pharmacist. "I moved on to greener pastures, but you know how it is. You're minding your own business and someone comes along and calls on you to come home and get involved in what really isn't any of your business, and what can you do, Bill? What can you do? Not responding is rude."

Bill? Marco had never once in his life called him by his first name.

Marco shrugged his shoulders. "Never once planned on being here again in my life. My work here was finished. I mean, okay, a couple of the Pageants lived through the day, but I was willing to let that pass. I got the majority of them and they suffered, Bill. They suffered right and proper before I put them down."

"The Pageants?" Bill's frown deepened. The only time he ever heard from the Pageants was when one of them picked up a prescription. Davey had a couple of anti-anxiety medications and both of his sisters were on birth control. Aside from refilling those prescriptions he virtually never ran across them, unless he was making a deposit at the bank and the twin who worked there was taking care of him.

"The Pageants, Bill. The Pageants. They murdered me, you know. Well, Earl did, but it was his property and I felt it best to go ahead and take it out on the whole family." He chuckled as he leaned in a little closer. "Now that I'm back, I'm going to take care of a few stragglers, Bill. The ones who didn't come out and play when everything got handled."

"Stragglers?"

"You sure do repeat a lot, Bill. Sure you aren't part parrot?" Marco leaned in closer still and Bill leaned back, unaware that he was doing it. Marco wasn't exactly scaring him, but he sure as hell was unsettling him.

"I repeat a lot? I mean, of course I do. You're not making any sense, Marco." There. That put paid to the situation. Marco was just being strange was all.

"I'm being cryptic, Bill. I like being mysterious." He let out a small laugh. "I mean, come on, how can you have any fun at all if everyone gets what you're saying? Take you for example. I've just pointed out that Earl Pageant was involved in a murder, and your response was to wonder what I was talking about, when you and I both know you were there when the fire happened."

"Fire?" Bill's stomach turned on itself and he felt the cold bloom there like he'd swallowed a massive ice cube and it was just in his guts, cooling him down from the inside.

"Don't be coy, Billy Boy. I remember you. I remember how you called out when the fire started. Was it you that actually barred the door, Bill? Or was that Earl?" Marco shrugged. "I couldn't really see who it was through the smoke, but I always thought maybe it was you."

Marco leaned back for a moment. "It's hard to remember perfectly, you know. Once my eyes started tearing up and the heat got bad enough to burn my eyelids away, I was basically just doing my best to see anything at all. That fire, boy, howdy, Billy, it got awfully hot in there."

Bill backed away, his hand reaching for the door, ready to lock the damned thing and keep Marco away from him, because Marco was too damned young to know about the fire. He wasn't even close to being born when the clowns got burned alive.

"I don't know what you're talking about. And, and don't call me 'Billy.'"

"Now, now, none of that." Marco came forward just as Bill started pulling the door closed. His foot moved fast and blocked the attempt to lock him out.

"What are you-?"

"Billy. Are you paying attention there, Bill? I said I'm back to take care of a few things. You're one of them." Marco moved closer and his foot shoved the door backward. Even as Bill reached for it again, Marco's hand closed on the edge of the door and hauled it wide open again. "You're not going to get away from me, Bill. Not now. Not ever. If you got on a plane right this instant and flew to another country, I'd still find you."

"I don't." His voice sounded whiny and Bill shook his head. He couldn't abide that notion. His hand reached for the .22 in his holster. "What do you want?"

"Well, I want a lot of things, Billy, I want my life back. I want my family. If I'm being honest, there was a girl in the freak show at the old circus who made my heart go pitter-patter and given a chance I'd give her at least one kiss. I think that's a good start."

The smile that had been growing broader and broader on Marco's face dropped away as quickly as a mask might fall. The expression that replaced it was cold and bitter and filled with hatred.

"I don't expect that's ever going to happen, Bill. I think those things that make us happy are fleeting. Or they can be, especially when they are stolen away."

Marco pushed into the room and Bill backed up with each step the young man took. Had he thought Marco was short? The man seemed to tower over him. Marco's hair was flopping wildly around his head, and his skin looked so pale in the light of the office that Bill thought he must surely be sick. The poor bastard was sweating fiercely.

"Your son? How old is he? Your little daughter? Do you have a daughter? I can't remember, Billy. I know you had a couple of kids. Marco knew that much."

"Marco knew? What are you talking about, Marco?" he shook his head. "It doesn't matter. I've called the police. You need to leave soon if you want to get away from them. They're coming for you and I don't think they're kidding around this time. I think they want you."

"Marco knew. Back when he was alive, Marco knew all about your family. I think he even liked you, despite you banning him from this dump." Marco moved toward him and as Bill watched, something went wrong with his skin. One second he had perfectly healthy-looking flesh and the next it was loose on his face and neck, like someone had slightly deflated a balloon in the shape of Marco.

"Gotta say, Marco wasn't a good kid. It didn't bother me at all taking his body." As he spoke Marco reached up and pulled at the sagging flesh, which tore away easily enough. Instead of seeing a bloody mess under there, for which he was grateful, Bill saw white skin, bright and clean as the whitest paint he'd ever seen, except where there were sudden splashes of color.

"What the hell are you?" He yelled the words. He had no choice, really. He was too surprised by the change to stop his mouth. Bill's hand reached again for the holster under his smock. Somewhere along the way he'd forgotten to grab the grip before, but not this time. Whatever the hell was wrong with the DeMillio boy, he intended to handle this matter until the police could show up.

The hand that caught his wrist was as white as the skin under Marco's face.

"No. None of that." Marco's face was different. The shape was the same, but there were marks carved into the startlingly pale flesh. Dark blue triangles were cut into his face above and below his eyes. A red slash of a smile spread beyond the full lips on that face, and a matching dash of red touched the tip of his nose. The dark curls of hair around his face framed and highlighted those changes. The eyes, so blue it was unsettling, looked down at Bill from what seemed like too great a height.

Fingers sank into his wrist and Bill let out a completely involuntary gasp as the pistol fell from his hand.

"You already killed me once, Billy. I can't have you doing that twice."

The bad part? The really, truly horrible part? Bill recognized the face. He had seen it only once before, back when he was barely a teenager. His dad had brought him along to show how justice was taken care of when the police failed to do their part. The clowns in that nasty old circus had been accused of doing horrible things to a couple of kids. The sort of stuff that should never be done to children.

Later, oh, later, they found out the truth. They found out about the sick bastard that had hurt the children. He'd been with the circus, yes, but he hadn't been a clown.

There had been tears. There had been prayers and, together, father and son had begged the Lord for forgiveness.

"Do you know what it feels like to burn alive, Bill?"

Rufo the Clown. That was the name. He remembered it even after all of these years. He'd been a circus clown and an escape artist, but he never made it out of the wagon. Bill's dad had seen to that. He'd barred the door with a heavy broomstick.

Bill shook his head.

"I do." The smile did not come back to that face, but the red grin was still there as a counterpoint to the angry snarl on the clown's face.

Bill shook. He tried to speak but all that came out was a whimper.

"Oh, relax, Bill. I'm not going to burn you." The smile came back to Marco's face. "It's been done already."

The deathly white hand not holding Bill's wrist reached out and caught hold of his face. The pressure was painful and he let out a yelp that became a full-on scream when the thumb of that hand dug into his left eye and broke through the delicate surface. He tried to get away, oh, how he tried to escape, but that hand was relentless and his eye became a fiery explosion of pain that would not leave him be.

"Doesn't mean this won't hurt, Bill." The clown was smiling again. That fact terrified Bill more than anything else he'd seen. "Trust me this is going to hurt a lot more than you can imagine."

The pain did not last all that long, but the clown was right. Bill had never felt anything like that in his entire life.

It was the last thing he ever felt.

Rufo was smiling when he left the pharmacist's office. The pharmacy was not busy. It was the early part of the day and while a few people were moving around on the streets, it seemed that shopping at the local Rexall wasn't really on their agenda just yet.

That meant the only person who saw him was the girl behind the counter. She looked up from her magazine with a smile starting to show on her face and then set the magazine down and frowned as he came her way.

Rufo slipped his hands into the pockets of his trench coat.

"Can I help you?" her eyes scanned him and her frown deepened.

He looked her over for a moment and shook his head. "No, thank you. I just wanted to say hello to Bill. We're old friends."

That was all it took to make her smile again. "Oh, okay then." Her smile opened broadly and he thought that she was even prettier when she let herself relax. "What's with the clown outfit?"

"You know, there's a gent down the road, Dave Pageant. He said he wanted to see Bill smile. Said Bill loves clowns." He smiled broadly. "You can never tell. Half the time people are terrified by the very notion."

She nodded emphatically. "Yeah, no offense but that's me. I'm sure you're a great guy, but that makeup is creeping me way out."

"Oh, no offense taken. Don't worry. I'm mostly harmless." He sighed. "I'd love to stay and chat, but I've got a list of things to do that practically goes on forever."

She nodded her head and if she looked a little relieved that he was heading out, that was only to be expected. Some people couldn't stand clowns. "You have a great day, okay?"

"Oh, it's off to a splendid start." He resisted the urge to wave. His hands were still coated with blood and she didn't need to see that.

A few hours later, the constables to come to see Dave a second time. He was at home and relaxing when they knocked on the door. The sun had just set and he'd finished with his chores on the farm only half an hour earlier.

As was his custom he'd showered after the work was done and felt better for it. The air was colder than he'd expected, which was foolish on his part, because it was almost Christmas, and he'd just cranked the heat in the farmhouse. The grates creaked and groaned and the warmth rose into the air even as he dried his hair.

He wasn't even considering the police when someone knocked on the door.

Dave looked directly at the nametag on Victor Barnes' heavy jacket and frowned. It took a few seconds before the sight properly clicked in his head.

"Hello, Constable Barnes. What can I do for you?"

"It's not Vic today?"

"It's not Vic when I think you're about to give me more bad news." Dave looked up at the man and shrugged. The cold air was brutal against his damp chest.

"Come on in, I'm freezing here." He moved out of the man's way and stepped back, giving lots of room.

Vic nodded and stepped through the threshold, quickly closing the door.

"What gave it away?"

"The lights on the car. If you were here just to chat, you wouldn't be flashing the red and blue."

Vic nodded.

"What's on your mind?"

"Well, we had another incident today."

"Incident?"

"Bill Kirby was murdered."

Dave stopped drying his hair and squinted at Vic. "Murdered?"

"He was killed violently. Beyond that I can't say much. It's an ongoing investigation."

"I'm sorry to hear that. I mean, Mister Kirby has always been a nice guy."

"You're wondering what it has to do with you?" Vic stood a little taller and then hauled his belt up a bit.

"I mean, yeah. I guess I am. It's horrible but I don't see the correlation."

Vic pulled out his I-Phone and thumbed past a couple of screens. He frowned, and used one of the preposterous fingers of his to find what he was looking for, and then showed it to Dave.

The screen showed a splash of blood across an old metal desk. He could see what looked like a hand on the corner of the desk, but far more importantly, he could see the massive letters scrawled across the wall in the same blood. They were hastily written and it looked like someone maybe used a finger as the brush.

They spelled out, "INVITATION ACCEPTED. SEE YOU SOON, DAVEY."

Dave stared at those words until the screen started to fade. Vic pulled his phone back. "I can't prove it's you one way or the other, but Kaley Hendricks, the girl who found the body, said the man she saw leaving was wearing clown makeup. Dark blue hair, blue triangles above and below blue eyes." Vic looked down at him and crossed his thick arms. "Sound like anyone you might know, Dave?"

There are people in this world who are designed to tell lies and those who simply are not. Dave Pageant was not good at telling falsehoods and he knew it.

"Sounds like Rufo the Clown." His voice was very low as he spoke. "He's sort of distinctive."

"Sort of." Vic nodded. "What did you do, Dave?"

Hard bands of pressure locked around Dave's chest and tried their best to ruin his ability to breathe. He wanted Natalie with him. Wanted to hold her in his arms and to feel her hug him back. She made him feel calmer.

"I don't know. I was trying to locate him. I have been trying to find him for a long time now, Vic. You know why." He looked hard at the bigger man. "You know why."

"I do, Dave. I know he killed your family. I was there when they were found." The constable looked at him for a long moment and then looked away. "I can understand why you'd want him found, but we don't have the luxury of denying what we already know, do we? That clown, he died a long time ago. Why were you trying to locate him?"

"He's not dead enough." Dave felt his lip pull down in a sneer. "He's not close to dead enough. I've got records showing that Rufo has shown up in Florida, Virginia, Atlanta, Washington, D.C., New York City, Kansas, Colorado, Arizona, and Hollywood. Those are the places with multiple sightings. Those are the places where people gave a detailed enough description that I thought I could trust it."

Vic opened his mouth to speak, his broad face slipping into an angry expression.

"No. Screw that!" Dave's voice was hard and Vic actually stopped trying to speak, his mouth set in a hard line. "Five years, Vic. Five years and no one anywhere came up with a solution. So I started looking on my own. Maybe I was wrong. Maybe I got something wrong, but all I did was call for the fucking clown so I could see him locked away."

"Okay. Locked away where?" the big man's voice was soft.

"What?"

"You said he's a ghost. Where are we going to have a ghost locked away?" Barnes looked at him with that same stern expression, but his eyes softened their glance. "Where do you imprison a ghost, Dave?"

"There's got to be a way. They show it in movies all the fucking time."

"There aren't any 'Ghostbusters' here." Vic crossed his arms and leaned down until they were roughly the same height. It was a feat. "So here's the thing, Dave. You tried to solve a problem and I get that. Near as I can figure, however, two people are dead because you decided to handle things on your own. Legally, you're in the clear. Nothing I can do to prove that you did anything. You will have alibis for everything that happened and there's no court in this land that would take 'dead clown did it because he got summoned, by a moron' as an actual crime." The man's fingers clenched and unclenched against his arms and Dave understood. He wanted to make fists and very possibly punish Dave for his actions.

He understood all too well.

"So what are we going to do, Dave? How should we handle this? I've got an A.P.B out for Marco DeMillio. He's wanted in several places and the thought that he might be alive is something that has to be considered." Vic stood back up and looked over his shoulder as the wind howled across the farm. "He's got a list of people in town he hates, you know. Not Marco, but the clown. Last I heard he sort of hated you for being a Pageant. I bet he hates your sisters, too, for the same reason. You might want to call them and let them know what you did. That way they can get out of town if they want."

"Can you put them under protective custody?"

"I can try, but if they don't want to be protected, or if the mayor decides that the town can't foot the bill for that sort of thing, well, it won't be a good time."

"Who else?"

"Who else what?"

"Who else is on his list?" Dave frowned. There were complications here that he'd never considered.

"For starters? Anyone whose family goes back in this area to the time when the circus got burned out and the bodies got hidden."

Dave frowned and shook his head. Hearsay was all that was.

"True story. The constables found notes written in blood and found a very serious and dark history of Serenity Falls in the house of Simon MacGruder. Remember him?"

"Yeah." Dave nodded.

"After he disappeared we searched his house. Found a dozen books of facts and stories that were mostly pretty easy to corroborate. One of those stories was about how the circus got burned right here at this farm.

"That history talked all about the bad things that happened here and the people who suffered. One of those names that came up was Cecil Phelps. He was a clown in the circus. Answered to Rufo when he was in makeup."

Dave's legs went weak. One thing to suspect something and another completely to have it pointed out as a piece of history.

"He wants everyone from that time dead, Dave, and you just invited him into the area. So what are we going to do about it?"

Dave licked his lips. "I could call the Parsons back in."

Vic shook his head. "I don't recall them doing much when they were here before. I know they came around and asked questions, but as I remember it Jacob Parsons wound up in the hospital and that was about all they accomplished."

"I can't call on him!" Dave's voice shook, not with anger but with fear.

"Yeah? Why not, Dave?" Vic loomed over him.

"Because he said if I ever did anything like that again he'd make me pay!"

"Anything like what, Dave? Come on, say it."

"He said if I ever called anything to this area again and it took a life, he'd take mine in exchange."

"Does that seem fair, Dave? Do you think you should get off the hook when you called a killer and invited him to come hunting?"

"I didn't mean for this to happen!" In his defense, Dave was angry and hurt. He was also a kid. Vic's expression said he was considering all of that.

"Nothing to be done about the past. I can't fix it. But I can give you this. You have to find a way to get rid of him. Send him away. If you can do that before anyone else dies, I can avoid making the phone call."

"He'll kill me, Vic." Dave's voice broke and he shook and the tears that ran hotly from his eyes shattered his vision into a million fragments.

"Okay, so we'll hold off, but we're going to have to find a way to stop the clown, Dave. I'll talk to him if it comes to that. No one's going to kill anyone if I have any say in the matter." The man's massive hand rested on his shoulder for a moment, but Dave took little comfort. If Jonathan Crowley came to town, he had no doubt in his mind the man would carry out his promises.

December 16th

Jack Michaels stared at his TV, looked at the moving images, but paid them little heed.

He was bored. He was always bored these days. That was the sad side effect of no longer being the chief constable. And that, in turn was the side effect of a massive stroke.

He could sit at home and watch TV. On a good day he could move his hands with enough dexterity to type. Most days he just watched and wished that the world had not answered his prayers with paralysis.

The apartment was big enough for his needs, and no larger. The staff at the Golden Trees Retirement Community took good care of him and he was sort of satisfied with his life.

He only wanted to kill himself on days ending with "Y," but he got over it pretty quickly. At least there were a lot of channels.

His right hand caught the remote and arrowed higher into the spectrum until he ran across Game of Thrones on HBO. The stories were dark. There was a lot of action and the beautiful girls never hurt his feelings.

It was all repeats, but that just meant the new season was starting soon.

He was watching the white-haired girl talking with one of the numerous men who wanted her. Something about going across the Narrow Sea, which meant she'd be off to conquer the world soon enough.

His face was faintly reflected on the TV screen and he looked past that as she spoke to the man and exerted her will. She was a beautiful girl no matter what the color of her hair. A shadow stretched out behind him, reflected in the TV screen, and though he was looking at the screen he couldn't quite make out the face that belonged to the shadow.

"When I was a kid, you gave me shit all the time. Always trying to make sure I stayed out of trouble."

Marco DeMillio's voice was soft. Still he recognized it.

He couldn't turn his head very much. But he could let out a moan. His lips were half-frozen in a snarl and his ability to speak was, well, limited, but he could definitely scream if he had to.

"It's not really Marco anymore. I'm Rufo. Marco died. I killed him when I came back." The voice stayed soft.

Jack's hand reached for the buzzer on his table. Rufo spoke very softly. "If you call anyone, I'll kill them. Do you believe me?"

Jack nodded as best he could and closed his eyes.

"Marco liked you. I know that's hard for you to believe, but he did."

Finally the shape moved, sliding around the edge of Jack's chair, the small table where he kept his remotes, and the buzzer for calling to the service staff.

The hand that moved the buzzer away was as white as snow. A moment later the man squatted until they were the same height.

"Listen to me. Marco liked you. I mean that. He liked you a lot. I don't much care what Marco liked or hated in this world. It doesn't have much of an effect on me. I can hear him if I want to listen and I can ignore him if I don't. Mostly I ignore him, but he's begging me to do right by you. And that after you shot me in the face. Do you remember that, constable? Do you remember killing me?"

Jack looked hard at the face in front of him. It was one that had been burned into his mind's eye a long time ago. Two bullets had hit the clown even as he had sliced open a woman's throat.

She'd lived. The clown had died. The clown took one bullet in the arm and another blew off the top of his head. Jack was pretty sure he'd hit the madman in the arm but he was hardly in a position to discuss the matter.

"You can't really speak, can you, Constable Michaels?" The eyes that looked into his were as cold as ice and a light shade of blue that seemed almost artificial. He remembered them well enough. They often frequented his nightmares.

The dead clown that he'd shot. The dead clown that, impossible as it seemed, had risen back from his place of death, had murdered Gene Halloway, and apparently eaten parts of the man, and then disappeared, never to be seen again, until now.

"That's okay. Here's my dilemma. I want you to suffer. I want you dead. Little Marco disagrees."

The clown smiled. His lips twitching past the red grin painted on his face.

"I think I have a solution. I'll just leave you alive, here, and let you deal with being stuck in that chair. I have a dime that says that's a bit like hell for you."

The clown nodded his head. "Yeah. I think that's a good choice."

He rose and looked down at Jack. "But don't you worry. I'll make sure to kill as many of your people as I can along the way. Marco gets to keep you. I get to watch you suffer. It's a good pay off."

Jack tried to clench his fists, but his traitorous flesh trembled and only left loose balls of flesh. He groaned, a deep and mournful sound.

Rufo stood up and smiled down at him. "Hold onto that anger. You have no idea how powerful it can be."

He took his time moving from the room. He paused several times to laugh at the situation, or maybe the impotent tears that fell from Jack's eyes were what had him so amused.

"So I've got to ask, I heard that twins can sometimes feel each other's troubles. Is that true?"

Amber had heard every come-on line on the planet. Or at least she thought so until she heard that one.

She looked up at the tall man that stood over her, his hands in his pockets and a winning smile on his face. Did he look familiar? Yes, but nothing clicked. He was just a cute guy with a bad pick-up line.

"You want to know if my sister feels it when I have a bad date? Or if she feels it when I have an orgasm?"

"I hadn't much thought about the orgasm notion." He chuckled deep in his chest and smiled at her. "Does she?"

"Not that she's ever told me."

"Well, I guess we'll have to do this the old-fashioned way." He shrugged as he spoke, and sounded genuinely disappointed.

Amber looked around the interior of Bailey's Burgers and frowned. It didn't happen all that often that she got hit on and genuinely felt uncomfortable, but she was heading in that direction.

"Look, nothing personal, but I only have a short time to eat before I'm back at the job, so if you could just let me have a little peace."

Instead the man slipped into her booth and smiled. He was quite handsome and there was something familiar about him but still nothing clicked. He was also exactly the sort of cocky prick she hated most in the world: Absolutely certain that he was the best thing going.

"No worries. I'm not trying to get closer to you so I can woo you."

"Woo? Really? People still talk that way?"

Not far away Brad Bailey was looking her way, like maybe he wanted to intervene and wasn't sure if he should. She cast a "please save me" expression his way and he nodded.

"Well, I'm an old-fashioned sort of guy. I hold doors for ladies, I make sure to take my hat off when I come inside, and I always get revenge on the families that kill me."

"What did you say?" her voice sounded wrong. Too soft. She could barely hear herself.

The interior of the place was deliberately left in semi-darkness. It let people have a sense of intimacy. Across the table from her the man's handsome face was half submerged in darkness, but his eyes nearly seemed to glow they were so blue. He smiled.

"I said sometimes I have to kill everyone in a family. I didn't want to, not really I thought I'd gotten my satisfaction and that I could leave a few of you alive, but, well, Davey has made that very difficult for me. He asked me here and I haven't been able to get him, or his twin sisters, out of my mind ever since."

"I. I don't want you near me." Her voice was still too weak. "I called the manager over. He'll be here soon to make you leave."

"What?" He snorted "Bill Bailey over there? Not a chance."

Brad chose that moment to come closer. "It's Brad, actually. Bill is my brother. I'm going to have to ask you to leave." Brad was wise enough not to touch.

"Hi, Brad. I'm Rufo. You should leave us alone before things get ugly." The man turned to smile at Brad, his teeth so very white, his lips spread in what seemed like an impossible grin.

Amber barely noticed. Her head was filled with a high, white sound at the name Rufo. She could remember the images of her family. She'd been the one to identify the bodies, after all. There had been a lot of them. Her mother, her father, her cousins her brothers and sisters. Her grandfather. So many dead that sometimes, when she was feeling too happy, their faces flashed before her eyes to remind her of the losses.

"You get away from me." She spoke calmly enough, but she reached into her purse at the same time and pulled out the pepper spray she had for emergency situations.

Meanwhile, Brad's heavy hand touched the stranger's shoulder.

Stranger? He'd basically just confessed to murdering her family.

"Amber, you want to call off your friend before this gets messy? Messier?" Rufo smiled. She fumbled the pepper spray out and took aim at the stranger who was a murderer.

"Fuck you. You're out of here." Brad was stronger than he looked. He'd spent his time in the Marines and he knew how to handle himself.

When he pulled on Rufo's shoulder the other man rose easily from his seat. Several other people around the restaurant were looking their way now.

Allen Halloway called out, "Take him down a few notches, Brad!" He was actually sounding rather cheerful.

Brad tried to wrench the other man's arm behind his back and found himself holding air. "Need to stay out of this, Bill Bailey. I mean it. I have no problem with you."

"Men don't hit girls or try to pressure them into anything. Not in my place."

"I'm not pressuring Amber into anything. I'm just going to kill her."

Amber took that moment to hit the bastard with pepper spray. The mist caught him full in his face and he howled as the pepper juice did its job.

Brad hauled the man backward, staggering, his hands over his face.

The two of them had almost made the door, her victim crying, when the man who claimed he was Rufo shifted his stance and danced easily away. His sounds of agony became the happier notes and he stood up, his clown face revealed, and howled laughter even as he reached for Brad. Brad blocked him and brought a knee up into Rufo's crotch.

The clown fell hard and stayed there, gasping. Brad reached for him again and the man slipped away, standing and smiling.

"Enough Brad. Final warning, I get it. I respect your code of chivalry, but for your own good, stop." He said the words through his laughter.

By that time three other men had risen from their seats. It's possible that in a lot of towns there would be no such motion, but they all knew Amber and they were all friendly.

Morgan Little was eating her steak with a knife. She stared at the clown as he reached over and plucked it from her hand.

When he moved again it was in an uneven line. He crossed to Walt DeWitt, who was just getting to his feet, and rammed the knife through the man's throat.

Walt fell back, both hands moving to the fountaining blood spitting from his neck.

Amber let out a small scream as the man who'd taught her high school English for two years fell back bleeding on the ground.

Rufo moved forward and caught Brad looking the wrong way. Brad, poor, sweet Brad, was reaching toward Walt, wanting to help as always, and Rufo caught his head and drove the back of his skull into a table hard enough to break the hard wood and Brad's cranium, too.

The next in line tried to run, whatever bravery he'd felt sliding away as the clown looked in his direction and then started moving.

"Nope! None of that, Rube! You wanted to play and now you have to pay the price of admission!" Ted Hendricks let out a yelp as the clown caught his hands and started bending his fingers back. One by one they snapped and Ted howled and still the clown kept pushing the issue until

Ted was on the ground, forced back onto his knees, his back arched and his hands held in a position of extreme pain.

Rufo nailed Amber in place with a glance and then did worse things to Ted, never once looking away from her. His gaze was pure hatred and madness and much as she wanted to move, she couldn't get her body to respond.

Ted let out an unholy wail of pain and then fell backward. His fingers were all crushed into new shapes, blackening and swelling already. The clown let him drop.

By that time the last man who'd risen to come to Amber's aid was gone.

Rufo looked at her and smiled. "Don't you fret. I'll find him."

"Leave me alone!" her voice broke as she screamed and she pushed out of her seat, away from her table, eyes wide and heart hammering.

The pepper spray hit the ground and rolled away from her.

The clown looked like it hadn't done a thing to him.

"I'm going to kill you, Amber. It's personal. I was going to let it all go, but your brother wouldn't leave well enough alone. I'm going to kill you. I'm going to kill your sister, and then I'm going to rip your little brother apart."

Rufo lunged then, his body popping forward like a spring-loaded dart.

When he hit her, Amber screamed and fell back, sliding across the tile floor and smashing into the closest booth.

Before she could even consider standing up he was there, reaching down and grabbing her by her red hair.

"Do you think your sister can feel this, Amber?" His eyes regarded her without any hint of emotion. Where he got the knife from she would never know, but she felt it start slicing into her cheek and then curve down toward her lips.

"I did this to Davey once."

She was too busy screaming to hear anything past that.

Dave listened to the news of Amber's death and nodded. He couldn't quite convince his body to move, but he could nod.

Natalie was next to him on the couch. They'd been talking, holding hands, and he'd found himself smiling for the first time in days, she could do that for him, and then Vic showed up and shit on everything.

Vic's words were supposed to be comforting but neither he nor Suzette cared. Natalie gasped when she heard the news and her fingers sought his, but he pulled away. He didn't want to, but he was going to need his hands. Not that it mattered. Not much of anything mattered except that Amber was dead.

Vic was very somber. "I'm going to call him. Dave. I have no choice."

Dave shook his head and reached into his pocket. The cell phone was where it was supposed to be.

He didn't have the number in his address book, but his fingers typed digits across the screen just the same.

The phone rang three times.

"Crowley. What can I do for you?" The voice was calm, professional and absolutely chilling.

"Mister Crowley? Hi, it's Dave Pageant."

There was a long pause. Then, "Dave? Did you do something wrong?"

"I guess I must have. Had a few deaths so far, too many. My sister." His throat tried to close up and he swallowed several times. "Amber. She's dead. Rufo killed her. It's my fault. I was trying to lock him away forever." Hot tears fell from his eyes

Crowley's voice was clear enough, almost pleasant, but he could hear the undertones through the connection. There was rage there, boiling just beneath the surface.

"Serenity Falls, Dave? Is that still where you are?"

"Yes. Still here. Still on the farm."

"I'll be there just as soon as I can. And then we're going to have a talk. Do you understand me?"

Dave nodded his head and gulped air. He couldn't seem to get a decent breath, no matter how hard he tried.

"Yeah. Okay. I'll be right here."

"Dave?"

"Yeah?"

"Disappointed doesn't even begin to cover my feelings. You understand that?"

Dave nodded slowly. "I'll see you soon, Mister Crowley."

He killed the call and sat back on the old leather couch where he'd watched TV when he was a kid. Across from him was the old piano where both his mom and his grandfather used to play.

Suzette called his name, but he didn't answer. He wanted to but he was too afraid.

Mister Crowley was coming for him. He didn't imagine he would survive the experience.

Vic reached down and wrapped that bear paw of a hand around his bicep and lifted him easily into a semi-standing position.

"Both of you are coming with me. You're going into protective custody."

"I don't want—" Suzette started to speak.

"I don't care." Vic said the words without malice. "You're coming with me, Suzette. No arguments."

He got none. Neither of the remaining members of the family were in much shape to debate anything at all. Natalie did not come with them. Instead she headed for home.

December 17th

Crowley closed the door as he climbed out of the car. "Don't go wandering away. I don't like this town and I don't want to be here." The car made no response but he didn't really expect it to. He just wanted it to listen this time.

It hadn't taken long to find out that the remaining Pageants were in custody at the station. They were both made as comfortable as possible, but there would be no chance that the dead clown could get to them without at least being noticed.

He looked at the oversized constable and nodded. The two of them got along just fine. Mostly because Victor Barnes was smart enough to call him when he was needed and to not piss him off.

In almost every case, Jonathan Crowley did people the kindness of removing their worst memories of a situation. That hadn't happened in Serenity Falls. There were too many people left alive and too many people left dead for him to consider a spell powerful enough to work through all the layers of interpersonal relationships. It would have taken him years to cast the spell properly and the people in that particular town had already been locked under a curse that lasted centuries. He didn't feel like doing anything else to their psyches.

He saw the older Pageant first. The girl had been crying and her eyes were red. Her lower lip trembled.

Dave looked almost as bad.

"So what? You thought I was joking when I said never to try that sort of shit again, Dave?"

Dave flinched as surely as if he'd been slapped. "I didn't mean to—"

"I don't care!" The boy was behind bars, which was one of the reasons Crowley didn't just slap the bejeezus out of him. "I told you what not to do and you did it!"

He stepped closer and pushed his face against the bars. "How's that working out for you, sweet pea? You having a good time?"

"He killed my family!" It was the only defense he could think of.

"Get over it!" Crowley scowled. "You think your mom and dad want you wasting your life like this? Get on with being a kid, you moron. You only get one chance."

In the next cell over Suzette chuckled softly. Her expression told him he was wasting his words.

"What did I say would happen if I ever caught you doing this again?"

"That I'd regret it."

"No. I said I'd make you suffer. Did you think I was bluffing?"

Barnes said, "Why don't we all calm down here."

"Shut up, Constable Barnes. I'm discussing serious matters with a very stupid boy." The words were said without malice. He could see Barnes frowning. He could tell the man wanted to respond, but was thinking better of it.

"I didn't mean to do it!"

"Yes, you already said that." Crowley stared harder. "Do you have any idea how often I hear that? It's like the 'I didn't know the gun was loaded' defense. It's crap! You were warned, Dave! You were told what would happen if you did anything again and you did it anyway! What the hell is wrong with you? I was looking for the damn clown. I've never forgotten about him. You asked for my help and I gave it then. What made you think I was going to stop any time soon?"

"Because you never got him! I was trying to find him and bind him and then I was going to call you." The kid looked wrecked and that suited Crowley just fine.

"And that's cost how many people their lives, buddy boy? Not just your sister, but a friend who trusted you and a few others who were just trying to help. Let's call it six people so far. Maybe more before this is done. You may as well have put a gun to six heads and pulled the trigger!"

Crowley's hands gripped the bars of the cell and he squeezed them hard, as hard as he could, to stop from reaching into the cell and slapping the foolish right out of the idiot staring at him and trembling.

"I didn't—"

"Still don't care! I'm going to fix this, Dave. I'm going to hunt that bastard down and take care of this, and when I'm done, I might even give you a head start before I come for you!"

Dave physically backed away from him as he screamed.

Good. The boy would maybe get it right this time.

"I'll be back just as soon as I'm done finding your clown, Davey. Just as soon. Until then the good constable and his team are going to try to keep you safe. We'll see if they have any luck."

Crowley turned and started away, his hands clenched at his sides.

Behind him Dave, and Vic, and Suzette all stared at the bars where his hands had been and at the dents shaped like his fingers and palms that now adorned them.

There was an all-points bulletin out for Marco DeMillio. Several people had even put up pictures of the face that existed before Rufo took the young man's body over and made it his. They had it all wrong, of course. There were similarities and if someone looked hard enough they could make the connection, but Amber Pageant proved that it wasn't always easy. For that reason, Rufo walked around the streets of Serenity Falls with impunity. All he had to do was put on a cap and change his coat and no one was the wiser.

It wasn't the features they remembered, it was the hair. If he wanted to, he could certainly cut that, but he'd grown rather accustomed to the longer locks as time had gone on.

Besides, at some point he'd want to be recognized again. There was no point to all of this if he had to wait around and remind people of why he was doing what he was doing. Dave knew, of course. The boy seemed positively obsessed, not that Rufo could blame him. You murder someone's family, you tend to expect a bit of attention from the survivors.

Dave was off the street. He'd dropped from the radar as a couple of bad cops shows had explained. He was missing in action.

Probably he was in protective custody. That was fine. He'd get to the boy, but first he wanted to cause as much pain as he could. The boy had to understand that Rufo was a threat. He had to know that when it came to clowns with an attitude, Rufo was in top form.

The girl was long and lean and pretty. She was never going to be beautiful, but she could certainly turn a few heads if she wanted. She was wearing baggy jeans and a loose-fitting sweater and her hair was hidden under a thick knitted cap with red and white stripes.

Rufo started walking, pacing along with her from the other side of the street, his heels clacking loudly on the sidewalk as she looked down at her phone and read a message; Occasionally her fingers would tap the screen in a flurry of activity.

He hated cell phones. They removed all of the personal connections between people and it could be said that Rufo believed people were better off with those connections.

Take a kid like Davey. If he'd had a few better connections, they might have talked the fool out of summoning Rufo to the town and Rufo might have continued to forget how much he hated the Pageant family for a few more years.

Sooner or later it was always going to happen. He'd made a promise to his dead friends that the town would pay and he meant to keep that promise. It was a point of pride, really.

The girl moved along at a steady clip and finally her attention to where she was. The store was called Second Time Lucky and claimed to have a collection of antique clothes. Back when he was a kid those were called hand-me-downs, not antiques.

The world continued to make ridiculously little sense.

He waited all of ten seconds and then crossed the street and entered the same shop.

The air inside the place smelled of incense and stranger things. In addition to a massive collection of used clothes there were also stuffed animals, plastic toys of every imaginable kind and posters that ranged from somber and moody to psychedelic. The music playing was from a band called the Grateful Dead. He'd heard them before. They were exactly the sort of music that would have enraged his father.

The girl was looking through a collection of coats, while the woman running the place was sorting through the newly acquired old clothes to resell.

She had done Rufo no harm and so he made certain to be quick about it. The girl, Natalie, barely had time to look up before the blade was opening the artery in her neck. He walked past her and pretended not to notice as she fell to her knees and then slumped against the rack of coats. Her blood painted the various fabrics in shades of red.

The woman who'd been sorting clothes frowned and looked over her cat rim glasses. She didn't bother with Rufo. She looked, instead, to the girl now falling on her face, her blood spilling across the thin carpet and soaking in fast.

"Young lady? Are you okay?" The voice was nasal and irritating. It became positively shrill when she took in the details surrounding the girl.

"Miss? Miss!" The lady moved, flowing from behind the counter with surprising grace. Her hand was already reaching for the cell phone in her apron.

Rufo slipped away, heading out the side door for the business and letting the bell ring shrilly after him.

Three minutes later the ambulance was on the way.

Two minutes after that the constable's police car showed up.

Rufo watched on and shook his head.

Pity, really, to hurt the girl. But Dave had to be taught his lesson. He had to suffer before he died.

Dave groaned deep in his chest and rocked back and forth when he heard the news. Suzette hadn't stopped rocking back and forth, but she cried fresh tears. Her boyfriend was over at the jail, checking in on her. Like as not he'd have stayed there with her if they'd let him, but the place wasn't designed to be a hotel.

Vic frowned, too.

He wanted to be out in the town and doing more, but he also wanted to make sure the Pageants were properly protected if the fucking clown came for them.

Dave made a deep moan of sorrow and rocked some more. Vic ignored him as best he could. The kid was still a kid, that was the thing. He meant to help, but he was just not as grown up as he wanted to be.

"If I had my papers, I could try to get rid of him."

"Not a chance. Even if I thought it would help, Crowley grabbed all the papers at your place."

Dave stood up and squinted in his direction. The kid wore contact lenses these days and his eyes were probably dried out. Vic made a note to get him some saline solution at the very least.

"You could get my computer. I have most of my files on there."

Vic was about to repeat his previous statement when Crowley spoke up from behind him. "You really think I'd be stupid enough to leave any files on your computer? Or that I'd be dumb enough to let you keep your computer? All of that nonsense is gone."

Dave's outrage fizzled even as it flared. His computer was gone? Not even a blip in comparison to the rest of his sorrows still there was an edge there. Grieving or not part of him wanted back what he's worked so hard to acquire, and Vic thought about what Crowley had said to him once about the nature of darkness. It's easy enough to feed. Just put the information out there for anyone to find and sooner or later someone would try to summon something to make their lives easier. That was why the man actively took away whatever source of information a person could find.

"Give me names, Davey. Who else do you care about that he might go after?"

"I don't know."

"Think hard, precious. The clown wants to make you suffer."

"He's doing a good job." Dave blinked away tears and tried to be strong.

Crowley shook his head. "Yeah, well, someone made it easy for him."

"What do you mean—" This time it was Suzette trying to stand up for he brother.

Crowley turned on her like a shark smelling blood. "No! You do not get to defend this little shit. If you'd been doing your job as his legal guardian this wouldn't have happened. You should have known what he was up to."

She said nothing else, but instead cowered in the corner of her cell, while her boyfriend held her. The boyfriend—Paul? Peter? He couldn't recall—looked about ready to wet himself. Crowley was smiling at him. That was normally enough to cause that sort of reaction.

"Who else, Davey? Don't make me ask again."

"Maybe Charlene Lyons or Jessie Grant."

"Why?"

"They were my friends back when everything was happening before."

"Were your friends?"

"They told me to quit, too. I wouldn't listen."

"Not all that bright after all, are you, slick?"

Crowley shot a glance toward Vic that was hard enough that he had to stop himself from stepping back. "Think you can find them?"

"Of course. It's still a small town."

"Well, I don't want to kill everyone. Not just yet." The voice came from behind him and Vic turned fast, his hand automatically reaching for the source.

Rufo slipped aside easily. The clown was smiling, baring his teeth, and he had service pistols in each hand. His eyes were blue and terrifying. His teeth looked like they had blood on them. His hands were stained crimson but the worst of the blood had been wiped away. His wild mass of blue, curly hair bobbed a bit as he raised the pistols.

"Do you have any idea how easy it was to take these from your constables?"

Without waiting for a response the clown opened fire on Vic. Unlike the clown, he didn't dodge in time.

Nine bullets slammed into his body and sent him staggering backward. Vic felt his weight crash into the bars of Dave's cage and then he slumped toward the ground.

He couldn't blink. He couldn't so much as grunt. Nothing was working as his world went gray.

In their cages, the animals were shrieking.

Crowley moved forward, his heart hammering.

He was immortal. That was his unique talent in the universe No matter what happened, he'd live through anything done to him. He was not bullets proof and sometimes healing took a while. Also, bullets hurt. A lot.

To prove his point, the clown got lucky and a high-velocity chunk of lead took off his left ring finger and the pinky, too.

Dave was screaming something incoherent and his sister was just plain screaming the man in the cell with her was pointing toward Victor Barnes and making an entirely different collection of noises.

Crowley was screaming himself, because his missing fingers hurt like hell and the clown was still aiming at him.

"Didn't expect to see you here again, Crowley, but you never can say what the world will offer." The clown was aiming one weapon at him and the other was pointing toward Suzette. Her boyfriend backed away from her, his eyes wide and his lower lip trembling. He didn't want to die. Crowley couldn't exactly blame him.

"Why don't you put the guns down and we can settle this the old-fashioned way?"

"I don't think that was the philosophy you used the last time we met, Crowley." The voice was strained, and the facial expression under the clown makeup was pure rage.

Crowley knew just how he felt.

"You tried to burn me alive."

"You got in my way!"

The clown opened fire. He didn't bother counting the bullets that hit him. Despite his best efforts to dodge, the distance was too short and Rufo was just good enough with his aim.

The first few wounds hurt enough to make him want to cry the bullet through his eye and the one through the top of his head took away the pain.

Dave stared on while the clown walked over to Crowley's body and kicked it a few times, experimentally, as one might test a tire.

"Hmm. Didn't expect that to work." Just to make sure, he unloaded the rest of the bullets from both of the weapons into the dead man and then dropped them on the floor.

"Well. Okay then. I guess we're ready for the main event."

Suzette looked at the clown and sobbed. Her boyfriend was no better.

Dave reached into his pocket and dug out the small patch of grave mold he'd scraped together. There was a spell for banishing ghosts, if he could just remember the words.

Rufo looked at him and smiled. There was nothing friendly about the expression.

"Seriously? You want to try magic on me? After all you've already screwed up?"

"I didn't screw up. I got you here, didn't I?"

"The binding ritual. Dropped the ball on that part, Davey. You got me here, but you didn't lock me away."

"I did that right. I know I did."

"Boy, I've escaped from death. I've actually escaped from hell. I've managed to escape every single place they've tried to put me. What makes me think you could hold me with anything you've learned in the last five years?"

Dave said the words and threw the small dose of powder at the clown.

He got something wrong. Nothing happened but the mold fell to the ground between them.

Dave stared at the block dust and shook.

"I'll kill Suzette first." Rufo turned his yes toward the girl, who was shaking her head and pulling at her own face with fingers that left red marks.

"No. The boy with her. Then her. He can be my practice run for her and she'll be my warmup for you."

"You don't have to do this."

"I was willing to leave you alone, Davey. Did you know that? I was willing to let bygones be bygones, but then you had to call me. Not just once, either." He wagged a finger and tsked. "I ignored the first few attempts. I get it. I understand all about pain, but you? You make stupid an art form."

"Fuck yourself!" Dave stood up and glared. Was he afraid? Not at that moment.

Rufo's smile grew a bit less intense.

"You have no manners at all, Dave. None. Your parents would be ashamed."

"You don't get to talk about them!"

"Who's going to stop me? Not you." Rufo frowned. "Not even a little chance of that."

"Yeah. Well. He brought help." Dave almost screamed at the sound of the voice, but he was too happy to hear it.

Around the same time he was talking, Crowley nailed the clown in his face with a vicious punch.

Rufo fell backward and tripped over the unmoving form of Victor Barnes. He got a comical expression on his grease painted face and then crashed to the ground.

The blood flowing from down Crowley's face almost made him look like a clown himself. He did not wait for the clown to get you, but instead threw a handful of dust at the dead thing and spoke his words.

Whatever he did was far more successful than what Dave had tried to do. The clown shrieked and writhed and crawled onto hands and knees as his skin blackened and began to smoke.

"Get it off! Get it off of me!"

Crowley smiled. The expression was as terrifying as ever, made worse by the crimson trails that marked his face.

"I burned too. Remember that? I do. You little bastard." Crowley's shoe slammed into the clown's side and sent him sprawling.

"Any chance of mercy went out the window when you *murdered* over seven hundred people!" Crowley hit the crawling form again as the smoke curled harder and darker and small spots of white-hot flame began to erupt on the clothes Rufo wore.

The clown looked up at him and sneered, sprang once again to his feet with the sort of agility that should never be allowed.

His hands caught Crowley at the throat and the man brought his arm around in a wide arc that slapped those hands away and left the clown open to a second attack.

Rufo looked surprised, but that expression switched to pain when the Hunter brought his other hand up and then down across both of the mad harlequin's arms and broke bones.

Still the fires burned, hotter and brighter as Rufo fell to the ground and groaned in pain.

"What is it with little freaks like you that makes you think you can do whatever you want for as long as you want? You're dead? You're angry? Too bad. I'm angrier and I don't like getting shot."

Crowley said more words that hurt Dave's brain and made him want to flinch. Rufo screamed in pain and the clown's face caught fire from the inside. The bones in that face flared white for an instant, so bright that the rest of the titanium white face seemed dull in comparison and then the flames vomited from the clown's mouth.

"Look away, Dave!"

Dave shook his head, and squinted, he wanted to see this. He wanted to watch every second of the clown's painful immolation.

The glare grew worse and even from several feet away Dave felt the heat that crinkled his hair and incinerated the dead thing that refused to die.

The sprinkler system in the area started up and the air was filled with the shrill screams of fire alarms. Water cascaded down from the ceiling and soaked him, but still Dave looked on, watched as Rufo fell onto his burning face and tried to scream. Flames continued to boil into the bastard's neck and then chest, and fire wrapped around him but spread no further. It wasn't the water, the water never even got close to the figure.

Crowley stepped closer to the flames and sneered down.

"Burn, you bastard. Just keep right on burning."

The smoke from the funeral pyre was thick and black and stank of sulfur and worse things. Crowley held out one hand and the smoke that should have been filling the room spun toward his open palm and flowed into a dark ball that rested impossibly in his grip.

Rufo screamed again, despite the fact that his lungs had surely burned away.

Blue afterimages covered both of Dave's eyes like cauls on newborn faces. Still he kept looking.

The flames grew brighter and surged and the heat was enough to steal Dave's breath.

Not far away Suzette screamed in fear and curled up into a ball with her boyfriend. Dave looked away exactly once to make absolutely certain that his sister was alive and then he watched on as the flames did their thing and flared into white streaks of light that ate bone, and spit out powder.

The smoke continued to pour into Crowley's hand and the powder on the ground sizzled and hissed as it cooled off.

A wave of Crowley's hand and the waterworks stopped along with the shrieking alarms.

"Burn. Burn and go to hell." Crowley kept staring at the incandescence until it stopped lighting up anything at all and all that remained of Rufo the clown was dust.

When it was done the man crouched and looked down at the ashes and then gathered them together into a pile. There was less than there should have been, near as Dave could see.

Maybe it was a magician's trick. Crowley moved his hands around that pile and slowly it vanished though he never seemed to pick anything up.

"That's it?" Dave could barely believe he was speaking.

Crowley skewered him with a glance.

"No. That's not it. That's one dead clown eliminated. That's seven people dead because you're too damned stupid to pay attention to me. Your sister. Your girlfriend. Both dead because you're an idiot."

Dave said nothing. He had no idea what to say and he was a little too scared of the man looking at him.

Crowley touched Victor Barnes and frowned. "He'll live. I can do that much."

Vic let out a deep moan and his limbs shuddered as if he were being electrified. While there was still blood on his clothes, the man looked healthier. Not healthy, but not as near death as he'd been.

Dave stared as Crowley headed for the door.

"Where are you going?"

"I've got some trash to dispose of." He held out his hands and Dave saw the mass of darkness that was held in his palm, a golf ball-sized storm of blackness that seethed and blistered the skin holding it.

"What about us?"

Crowley scowled. "What about you? Do you really want me coming back? I was thinking maybe you've suffered enough, but if you'd like I can give you the same treatment. You're just as guilty of murder."

Suzette spoke up. "No! He's fine. He's just fine. And thank you." That last part faded almost to a whisper as Crowley looked her way.

"Davey, I'm going to be watching you. I even think you're looking at a book on haunted houses and I'm coming back." He stepped closer and glared at Dave, that damnable smile of his showing up once again. "You get me? You understand what I'm saying?"

Dave nodded. His bladder throbbed with a need to pee, but he didn't dare move. The eyes on his seemed too large for the face they were in and once again tears threatened.

"You never let me think about you again, boy. Or by God I'll make you suffer."

Crowley turned and walked away then, heading for the door to the detention center and whatever might lay beyond it.

The floor was wet here and there, but there were no scorch marks to prove that any sort of fire had burned.

Suzette was crying. He could hear her sobs.

He couldn't make himself look. He might start crying himself.

Crowley walked out into the cold air and clenched his fists.

In the palms of his hands the essence of a demonic clown shivered in pain and that brought a smile to his face.

Not far away a woman who had no idea at all what had happened flinched and started away, unsettled by his expression and fairly convinced that he would do her harm.

Behind him the last two members of the Pageant family stayed locked in cells.

He didn't care. They could rot away for a decade and he'd feel no guilt. There were some sins he could not forgive and while the girl has not done as much wrong, she'd let those sins be committed.

He was tired. These days that always seemed to be the case.

Crowley cast his eyes around the town of Serenity Falls, and hoped he'd never have a reason to visit the location again. It was the site of one of his greatest failures and he'd just as soon not remember it.

The pain in his palms reminded him to bond the damned spirit and cast it away.

The process only took a few moments and, when he was finished, the burning sensation was gone and so was all that remained of Rufo the Clown. Dead once again and forever.

"That's it. I'm done here."

He walked toward the car that waited exactly where he'd left it, and scratched at his palm. There were places he needed to be and he wouldn't get there by dawdling in locations that still haunted him.

Little Boy Blue

The problem, near as anyone could tell, was that someone wanted the Bloome family dead. Not too surprisingly, the family in question wasn't excited about the idea.

Three weeks earlier, Leon Bloome had been a healthy, happy twenty-seven-year-old man with the world ahead of him, a career in the pharmaceutical industry effectively guaranteed to him, and a fiancé that most men would gleefully kill to spend an afternoon with. He'd have told anyone who wanted to listen exactly how lucky he was, too, because he'd been raised to appreciate the value of the life he had been granted.

Two weeks ago, he'd have been a bit doubtful. That was after seven days spent suffering from aching joints, slightly blurred vision, a deep and continuing inability to catch a decent breath, and a heartbeat that refused to stay steady.

One week after that, he'd have told anyone who asked how miserable he was, and damn the money and everything else, because little seemed to matter anymore but the pain. His hair was falling out, his eyesight was shot to hell, his breaths came in an endless series of gasps and wheezes and four of his perfect teeth were loose in their sockets.

Doctors were called, tests were done and studied by still more doctors who took notes and tried to find comparisons to other, previous cases. There was no viable discernible reason for the illness, despite worries of everything from cancer to radiation sickness. Heavy metals were tested, every poison the professionals could think of was considered, and because the family had the money to cover the tests, still more specialists were called.

By the time Leon passed away, the rest of his family were getting worried. Not only because their loved one had passed, but because he was the fourth member of the family to die from the unusual illness. No two people ever suffered the symptoms at the same time, but as soon as one died, the next in line took ill.

Under most circumstances, the family would have considered a few alternatives, such as moving away from the family home or locking themselves in a safe environment, but the situation wasn't that easy. Dennis Bloome, nineteen and studying pre-law in Black Stone Bay's Winslow Harper University, was the first family member to fall victim. He'd been in upper state New York when the illness hit him, attending a seminar just outside of Utica when the symptoms that eventually caused his death started to present themselves. All while sitting in a room with fifteen other people who were not affected.

Dennis's death took place in a hospital in that area, and due to the extreme nature of the illness he was not allowed any visitors, even family. Even the doctors and medical staff had taken to wearing contamination suits, just in case whatever virulence was attacking him managed to be an airborne contagion.

Two days after his unfortunate demise, Laurence Bloome, forty-two, fell into the same series of symptoms. He was on a trip to London at the time. Despite the excellent care he received, he died three weeks later with no one the wiser as to the cause of his troubles.

Angela Bloome, age eighty-three, was the next to fall victim. She suffered from all the same symptoms but died before she reached the hair loss stage. By that point some of the family members were beginning to doubt whether or not there was a medical reason for the strange occurrences. Most of the suspicion fell to the various black sheep of the family, but even the worst of the lot couldn't jump from continent to continent without being seen and three different private investigators were doing their best to track the movements of every sibling, cousin, aunt, uncle, nephew and niece in the entire lot by the time Angela passed away.

The detectives cost a small fortune and learned remarkably little, except that there were no noticeable connections between the deaths. That is to say, aside from the fact that every person involved died under the same unsettling circumstances, there was remarkably little in common and as far as they could tell, none of the less savory family members were responsible for the unexplained deaths.

As Leon Bloome breathed his last in an isolation ward, his mother, Anita, talked to her best friend from college, one Laurie Masterton, on the phone. Even as the first family members were being notified that he was deceased, Laurie dug in her purse and finally managed to find a scrap of paper she'd always kept nearby.

"Anita, honey, you know Leon is in my prayers. Your whole family is. Now, I want you to do me a favor. I want you to call someone for me."

"Call someone? Is he a specialist?"

"Do I need reference? Would it be better if you called him first?"

"Oh honey, no. I love you to pieces, but I can't talk to him again."

"Oh. Is this one of the guys you used to date?" She asked the question carefully. Not only because Laurie was happily married now, but because she left a trail of ruined men behind in her earlier days and did her best to forget that she had been a complete bitch when she was in her prime.

"Oh, no. No, this isn't one of my exes. I met this one after we graduated."

"So he's an ex?" sometimes Laurie could be vague. It was one of the things you just had to accept if you were going to be her friend.

Just the same, much as she loved her sorority sister, an edge of annoyance had crept into Anita's voice and Laurie got it. "No. He can help you. It's just... I can't talk to him again, Anita." Her voice broke into a whisper. "He scares the hell out of me. You can give him my name if you want, but I can't talk to him."

"And you think he can help me?"

"Honey, if science isn't doing it and the detectives aren't catching anything, he's your next bet."

Anita took the number and held back from stating her doubts about the situation. Laurie was smarter than she acted. And there was no reason to doubt her advice now. After a few more minutes of talking -of not watching her oldest boy dying for no known reason- she got off the phone and made the call.

She was about to hang up when a voice suddenly answered. "This is Jonathan Crowley. What can I do for you?"

Anita started talking, sporadically at first, but soon she was explaining everything to the man on the phone and he kept guiding her through with simple questions and a patient tone of voice.

When she had answered the questions she felt like she was coming out of a deep sleep and she shook her head as he spoke his last words before disconnecting the call. "I'll be there as soon as I can. Don't start the fun without me."

Jonathan Crowley flipped his cell phone shut and let it fall into the passenger seat. The car was quiet for a change, but only because the station he'd been listening to had faded away as he crossed over the last hill and he hadn't started searching for another oldies station before the call came through.

"Now I'm getting references. I swear, I should require invitations and RSVPs." His voice was low and cranky, which most people who'd met him would have explained meant he was in a fairly good mood.

The road was dry, but it didn't look like that would last too long. He was currently heading toward a sky that was black and grey and promised wind and rain with every distant flash of lightning that lit the distant clouds.

That was okay. Crowley was feeling a little like the pending storm at the moment. Now and then the promise of violence on the horizon made him feel better and he could feel the start of a smile playing at his lips.

An old family where members were dying one after another even when the members were hundreds of miles apart, almost guaranteed he was dealing with a curse, unless the situation was more mundane than he was expecting.

Normally people didn't call him until they had run out of options. Even then, they hesitated. He preferred it that way. With very few exceptions no one called on Crowley for social reasons. He was not a social sort of creature and hadn't been for a long time now.

An eighteen-wheeler on the left of him swerved slightly and he compensated. Despite the temptation to make an obscene gesture, he held his own. He didn't have all the facts yet and that meant it wasn't the proper time for reacting.

The phone rang again and after making sure the trucker with the loose steering wheel wasn't going to switch lanes, he answered it.

"This is Jonathan Crowley. How can I help you?"

"Mr. Crowley?" He recognized the voice immediately he'd only been speaking to the woman a few moments earlier.

"Yes, Ms. Bloome? How can I help you?"

"My son, Leon, he passed away." Her voice broke into a series of faint subs and Crowley scowled.

Guilt? A small twinge, but very small. He'd only just taken the case and he was hardly a miracle worker.

"I'm so very sorry for your loss, you have my condolences."

"Mr. Crowley, unless something changes very soon, either I or one of my family will be dead within the next three weeks, unless you can stop whatever is happening." She spoke calmly, but he could still hear the tremble in her voice, the desire to fall apart and let herself get lost in grief.

"I'm well aware of the stakes involved, ma'am. I'm still currently on my way to your address. I'd recommend that you gather as many of your family together as you can, the better to expedite whatever I might be able to do for you."

"You want us all together?" Her voice gave away her surprise at the notion.

"Absolutely."

"Why?"

"Because that way I might be able to see who's afflicted next and I might be able to stop it. Also if someone in the family is responsible, I might be able to tell that too."

"Mister Crowley, my family is rather large, it's been quite some time since we had a reunion—" The tone had changed, one-part explanation, two parts exasperation.

"Then I recommend you start making potato salad, because it's long overdue."

"I don't think you understand the magnitude of your request."

"You're grieving, so I'm going to be polite. Get them together. Tell them it's a matter of life and death, theirs. That's all. I'll be at your place by tonight, maybe a little after sunset. By then, have as many of your family there as you can manage." He hung up the phone and accelerated. The truck was still too close to him for his comfort and it was wobbling again. When he'd successfully passed the vehicle he relaxed a bit.

The truck swerved to where he had been a moment before, the driver steering like a mad man to avoid having the entire rig jackknife on him.

Crowley accelerated again, just in case, and caught sight of the car in the farthest lane, that had been effectively hidden by the truck until that moment.

"You've got to be kidding me..."

The man driving the little white car was swerving all over the place, and badly enough to have a trucker get worried about his safety.

Crowley shook his head and accelerated a bit more. He kept an eye on the car as best he could, because he didn't trust the man not to get him killed. Better that the idiot be in front of him, but any distance would do in a pinch.

He went back to contemplating his latest case. "Family curse, has to be. But what has the family been doing to piss someone off that badly?"

The car did not answer him, so he started the search for a decent radio station again. While he was distracted the idiot in the white car almost creamed him. A loud horn honked and distracted Crowley from his quest for a good classic rock station. He looked up from his fruitless search just in time to see the car swerving and to realize that he'd slowed down. He shifted lanes effortlessly, cursing under his breath, and looked murder at the driver of the other car. The man was on a cell phone, chatting away as he balanced a coffee in one hand and a sandwich in the other. He looked at Crowley and waved a casual apology, oblivious to how close he'd come to dying.

Crowley opened his mouth to let loose a flow of obscenities, but instead nodded his head and slowed down. Sooner or later the idiot would stop. That was when he would deal with the matter.

The trucker shook his head in sympathy and Crowley waved a quick thank you for the save. Hardly the sort of man he'd normally have an intellectual discourse with, but the driver had saved him a few hours of painful recovery at the very least.

A little over an hour later the white car pulled into a truck stop and almost immediately into the full-service line for fuel.

The fuel gauge in the car hadn't changed, yet Crowley pulled off to the side. He could wait if he needed to.

That was the one thing about being the Hunter. He'd learned a lot about patience over the years.

The mind was sharp, but now and then George Cambrio's body betrayed him. He told the kid at the pumps to fill the gas tank and then he slid out of the car seat to stretch his legs and empty his bladder. For the first time in over an hour, he took the phone from his ear and relaxed a bit. Being a salesman meant living on the road way too often, and that in turn meant living with the phone almost glued to him.

The truck stop was busy and the people inside were all looking a bit harried. Everyone everywhere was in a hurry these days and that was something he could understand all too well himself.

There was a waiting line to get into the men's room, but he had no choice in the matter. Either he was taking a piss, or he'd be buying some adult diapers to finish his trip.

The line finally got moving as George broke into his version of the Gotta Pee Dance, left foot, right foot, left foot, right foot, clench bladder hard and repeat as necessary.

He found a urinal without too large a puddle in the front of it and unzipped his pants just in time for the phone to go off again. It took effort, but he managed to answer the phone and take aim with his free hand at the same time.

"This is George, what can I do ya for?" His voice was as cheerful as ever.

So was the voice behind him that spoke even as a hand snatched the phone away from his ear.

George started to turn, completely forgetting the stream of urine that would no doubt bathe whoever was around him, but a hand shoved into the small of his back toppled him into the urinal proper. Before he could fall too far, he caught the wall and grunted, trying to push himself back into a standing position, but it wasn't working. Whoever was behind him was simply too strong. "Hi. No, no, George is a little indisposed right now. No, actually, he's taking a leak. Yes, he's peeing. Disgusting isn't it? Trying to talk to you on the phone while he's taking care of business, as it were."

He tried to turn around, but whoever was holding him in place was out of his sight and there wasn't a damned thing he could do about it. The stream of urine sprayed the porcelain and the backsplash wet the front of his slacks. George let out a squeal of protest but couldn't escape from the position he was in.

"No, he'll call you back in a few minutes. He has some unfinished business to take care of with me."

The pressure faded from his back just as George was starting to seriously panic, and he pushed away from the wall as his bladder gave off the last few drops, which leaked freely down his leg.

"What the hell is wrong with you!?" He didn't bother looking first, but cut loose with the anger. Some sick bastard had just humiliated him and made him piss himself; there would be hell to pay.

The man standing a few feet away from him and holding his phone was grinning ear-to-ear, with what had to be the craziest smile he'd ever seen. Not happy crazy, but scary, psychotic, I-eat-babies-for-lunch-and-their-mommies-for-dinner crazy.

George stared hard at the broad smile and the plain face that surrounded it, and felt another trickle run down his leg.

"What's wrong with me?" The man was average, almost painfully so, except for that mad grin. His hair was brown, his eyes were brown behind rimless glasses, even his clothes were so damned plain as to fade into the woodwork. He tilted his head a little as he studied George, and then he held out the cell phone he'd stolen. "Wrong with me?" he repeated. "Nothing! Not a single thing. I was going to ask you the same question a little while ago, you know, when you were on the phone and talking to who-knows-who while you were eating your fucking lunch."

George frowned, at a loss.

"You know, when you almost knocked me off the road after you almost sideswiped an eighteen-wheeler." The man stared at him, waiting for some sort of acknowledgement. George shook his head. He wasn't about to give the man the satisfaction.

"I don't know what you're talking about, mister." The look of shock on the man's face was enough to make George take a chance and reach for his cell phone.

The man shook his head and yanked the phone out of his reach. "Un-uhn. Not a chance, sweet pea."

"That's my phone."

"Nope. It *was* your phone. Now it's mine."

"But I paid for it." He felt a slow panic starting in his chest. His phone was his connection to clients, to the home office, to, well, everything that mattered in George's world.

"Yes you did. And when you almost killed me, I decided you couldn't be trusted to play with it anymore." The stranger spoke in patronizing tones that did nothing to help George's disposition.

George's chest felt tight and he blinked back tears of frustration. He wasn't an overly large man, but neither was he small. Most of the time he was the one who managed to convince people to back down from fights and it had been a very, very long time since anyone had threatened him with any sincerity. Most people were simply too civilized. But the man standing in front of him was the exception to that rule.

He wanted to swing, to take back what the man standing only a few feet away had stolen, and to retaliate.

And he would have, if he hadn't been so damned scared.

The smile on that plain face grew broader, more intense. "That's what I thought. Got no guts. Go on, go back to your car, precious. I'll keep the phone to stop you from getting in any more trouble."

George stared hard at him, willing the man to give him back his phone. Instead, the stranger turned sharply on his heel and walked out of the restroom. He didn't run. He walked. Slowly.

George tucked himself back in his pants and then washed his hands, praying silently that the man would be gone when he was done making himself presentable.

The stranger was gone, along with George's cell phone. He couldn't decide if he was happy or if he should cry.

Crowley stood on the side of the road and watched the police dig through every nook and cranny of his car with only mild interest. They'd never find anything in there, first and foremost, and the delay was annoying, but hardly fatal. Well, not for him at least.

Georgy-Porgy-Pudding-and-Pie with standing next to the cop car and looking less and less confident by the second. After several minutes of searching -including taking out Jonathan's suitcase and sorting through the clothing and toiletries inside- Officer Hamilton shook his head. "There's nothing out of the ordinary here, sir."

Crowley nodded his head and crossed his arms. "As I said, I've never seen that man before, except a little earlier on the road when he almost cut me off when he switched lanes."

The cop's eyes were hidden behind reflective sunglasses. All Crowley could see was his own sincere face staring back from the glass on the lenses. Just the same, the man's lips pressed together as he nodded curtly.

"I'm very sorry for the trouble, sir."

Crowley shook his head and let himself flash a very small smile. "Not to worry, Officer. You're just doing your job."

The two parted company and Crowley quickly placed his suitcases back into the trunk of his antique Charger.

The officer went to have a long chat with George, who was looking decidedly uncomfortable by the time Crowley left.

He watched in the rearview mirror and smiled to himself as the cop tore into the traveling salesman. As if he'd have kept the damned phone in the first place. It was back at the truck stop, turned off and rusting in a trash can. He had better things to do with his time than to take messages for an idiot.

After that it was back on the way to his latest case, and happy for the brief distraction.

He arrived at the Bloome house a little after eight in the evening. The place was old and well kept. The only thing missing to make the image of an Old English manor complete was a proper wall of fog and moors for said fog to obscure. The land was pristine, well-groomed and plentiful. The house itself could have held fifteen people comfortably without any worries about them getting on each other's nerves.

Despite the cheerful distraction of a few hours earlier, Crowley was in a dour mood when he pulled up. The house was the sort that could hold too many secrets, old enough to almost guarantee that he'd be busy for a while trying to decide what was behind the curse that he suspected was behind the recent deaths. Also, judging by the number of vehicles in front of the sprawling residence, the family reunion was well underway by the time he got there.

"Blue bloods. Of course they're blue bloods." He shook his head and scowled once more before composing himself. It wouldn't do to make a bad first impression. Well, at least he didn't want to make one that was any worse than the usual for him. He was not a people person, not even in his wildest imaginings. He was a loner and he preferred it that way. He was, to date, the only person who hadn't let him down too many times to count.

The door was answered quickly by a heavyset woman in her mid-forties. She looked at him blankly for several moments as if she expected there to be more to him. Finally, she responded with, "Yes? May I help you?"

"I'm looking for Anita Bloome. She should be expecting me."

"Anita?"

She was grieving. Possibly. Maybe she was just stupid, but he had to assume it was grief that was making her into an idiot.

"Anita Bloome. I believe she lives here. She invited me to help with the family's current situation." Patient and calm. He made sure he stayed patient and calm. Deep slow breaths helped.

Finally, the vapid woman's eyes widened. "Oh dear. I thought you were the caterer."

"I'm sorry. I thought the lack of a chef's outfit, catering truck for chafing dishes might have explained that possibility away."

She looked at him for a moment, taken aback by his comment. "I'll just go see if Anita is ready to see you then." The frost and her voice did nothing but amuse him.

"Thanks. If I see the caterers, I'll give you a holler."

Crowley looked around the exterior of the building as casually as he could while he waited for his hostess. There were numerous cars along the substantial driveway and not a one of them was actually an economy model. The Bloome's were not suffering in the current recession. More power to them, unless, of course, they'd been stupid in acquiring their wealth.

There was always the possibility that they'd been dealing with demonic influences to get their wealth and to keep it. Hardly a first in Crowley's experience, but definitely one of the best ways he knew of to screw over a perfectly good life.

Once a demon decided to attach itself to a family, it could feed on them for a long time, provided the family in question didn't run out of fresh blood. Of course, at the current rate of consumption, the demon would run out of numbers within a few years, which was why he suspected a curse instead of a bargain with a hell born entity.

Even the dumbest demonologist didn't normally screw their entire family over in an attempted bargain. Demons were not what most people expected. They might appear as a goatman with horns, but it was only the way they chose to show themselves. They were energy beings and they might feed on human souls, but what most of them wanted was access to a place that was less hellish than what they usually called home. In exchange for that access, they could be convinced to grant wishes, kill enemies or any number of other boons. But the person summoning them had to be very, very good at what they did if they wanted to stay alive for more than one or two bargains. Demons could and would take any chance that presented itself to stay away from Hell and stay in the material world. Having been to at least three separate hells to date, Crowley couldn't really blame them.

He pushed the thoughts away as the brunette came back with another woman in tow. Anita Bloome looked to be in her mid-forties to early fifties, with light brown hair that was silvering nicely and a body that was kept in shape by several natural means. The woman's muscles were well-defined, but her breasts were showing her age, as was the line of fine freckles around her eyes and along her neckline.

She was also a very attractive woman and Crowley noted it. He wasn't looking, but he could appreciate beauty when he encountered it.

"Mister Crowley?" The lady's eyes were tear-stained. He could understand why.

"Ms. Bloome. I'm sorry again for your loss."

"Leon was a good boy. He will be missed." She held herself together. When most of the people he knew would have been bawling like babies and fully justified in the act, the woman held herself with the sort of regal bearing that few outside of old money families seemed to manage. It was a trait he admired, but not one he often bothered with.

"I need to see everyone in your family who has gathered here. I need to see all of them, and preferably together. It doesn't have to be right away, but it should be fairly soon, within the next day or so. I also need access to any historical documents the family might hold."

The woman nodded at the first part of his request, doubtless expecting as much from him, but frowned lightly at the second, as if he were making a frivolous suggestion.

"Why would you need to see a collection of old notes?"

"Because in my experience when there's a family issue, it normally has its roots somewhere in the family's past."

He didn't know the hierarchy of the family in question, but either as a result of her grief or simply her station within the family, Anita Bloome was in control of the situation. She handled it with exactly the sort of grace he would have expected after meeting her. "Dora? Would you kindly escort Mr. Crowley to the library and show him the family papers?"

Dora, the portly brunette, nodded her head vacantly for a moment and then turned back to Anita. "All of them?"

"Of course." With the smallest change in her expression, the grieving mother chastised her relative. "He's here to stop whatever is causing us harm. We're going to do everything we can to help him in his attempts."

Crowley offered a brief nod and followed the other woman to the library, which was every bit as large as he'd expected.

There were sections within the oversized room for law books, medical journals and almost every science known to man. He was rather surprised to find one of his earlier works on botany among the books. Pleased enough, true, but more surprised than anything else.

Dora showed him to a table and promptly started hovering. He ignored her for several minutes but she still hovered.

"I'll be here for quite a while." He cast a sharp look at the woman, who set her face like stone and crossed her arms. After a moment, he shrugged. "Suit yourself."

After almost two hours of being pointedly ignored, the woman finally took the hint and left him in peace.

Crowley settled in to read. There was a great deal of history for him to attend to when it came to the family and most of it was as exciting as watching condensation form on a glass of ice water.

The night grew long in tooth and eventually became early morning. Crowley continue to read, sorting through the histories of the family as told by people who lived it. Sometimes they were skilled writers, but more often they were merely decent accountants. From time to time he stood and stretched, but more often than not, he's simply sat and continued reading, not bothering with notes.

A little after seven in the morning, Anita Bloome came into the library, no doubt fully expecting to find Crowley asleep. Instead she found him setting down another piece of the family history and staring at the wall of books across from him.

"I thought you might like coffee, or perhaps breakfast?" She stared at him, and though she hid it fairly well, he could tell she was disconcerted. Most people tended to look like shit after an all-night study session. He felt perfectly fine and knew he looked about the same as when he'd arrived. There was no need to pull out hair or let his clothes get disheveled when he was reading. Just as she held in her grief, he held in his inner slob.

"I'd love breakfast. As a matter of fact, I was just finishing up here."

She nodded her head sharply and refrained from asking him anything. He chose to be cruel and not answer her unasked questions. There was still a little more he needed to know.

Besides, he hated repeating himself and there were a lot of members of the Bloome family that were going to have similar questions.

The family drifted into the dining room, a large affair that had been set up with several tables and a generous selection of different foods. A few people were down and eating, but more of them showed up as he poured himself a cup of coffee and chose a bit of this a little of that to qualify as his breakfast. By the time he'd settled into a seat, he could fully understand the need for a caterer and for the large dining area. There were close to thirty people staying at the home or visiting the residence and it was still early enough that he suspected there would be more before it was all said and done.

He ate alone. Several people took note of him, but no one approached. That gave him time to study them, which was for the best.

They were, to a person, well tutored on how to behave. He had seldom seen a family so completely devoid of bad manners. Most of them might have considered misbehaving in front of family, but certainly not in front of a guest and most decidedly not under the circumstances.

He resisted the urge to belch as loudly as possible, but only out of respect for Anita. Most of the people in the room struck him as the sort that would annoy him on general principles: too much money, too much idle time on their hands, and far too little actual life experience under their collective belts. Old Money tended to cause that sort of problem after a while. He knew, because there had been a time when he was just as pathetic.

They milled about and ate their food and finally, when he could sense them getting impatient with the stranger among their ranks, he walked over to Anita where she sat surrounded by family and asked if she was ready for him to talk to her brethren. A very courteous and polite "Yes, please," was the response.

Anita stood, and the general murmur that had built the room was stifled within seconds.

"Everyone, I have a guest here today. This is Doctor Jonathan Crowley. He's a specialist. He believes he knows what is happening to the family, what has brought misfortune to us, and what we can do to stop it." Her voice was steady and strong as she spoke, but she wrung her hands with strained nerves as she looked from one family member to the next.

Crowley waited until she seated herself again and started speaking, his voice naturally sliding into lecture mode. Years as a college professor had taught him how to project, and he had no doubt that every person in the room could hear him.

"I've spent most of the last twelve hours poring over the Bloome family history. It's an interesting one, to be sure." That elicited a few chuckles, which was what he'd expected. "To start with, your ancestors came here on the Mayflower, a fact I suspect you already know." A nod or two, plus a few interested expressions. "Aldridge Bloome made a fortune for the family, his descendants lost the fortune. Eventually, they recovered enough to keep the family together. Richard Edward Bloome inherited a small lot of land from his father. He took his time and made wise choices in investments, went to university and worked himself silly. The end result was the house you're currently standing in and the start of the family fortune. His sons were shrewd businessmen. They managed to take what their father had built and expand it substantially."

Crowley looked around the room. None of the people listening to him were unfamiliar with the family history. They might not have known all the names and dates, but they most decidedly understood that their fortunes had been established in the past.

"Then, when things started going the wrong way in this country, the Bloome brothers worked out a few deals for transporting wine and alcohol during prohibition and stored their money away. When everything calmed down and the markets were looking better, they invested in land.

Most of the family fortune is still in real estate, though a nice sideline in pharmaceuticals and a string of lawyers in the family have kept things sailing smoothly over the decades."

A blond man, late forties, with a paunch and two chins shook his head. "With all due respect, Crowley, we don't need a history lesson."

"But you do, Mr. Bloome. You most definitely do. Just certain parts of the history, really." Now Crowley smiled. He was warming up to his subject and the idiot who'd spoken out of turn gave him a target to deal with.

"For instance?" Blondie was looking positively bored.

"Little Boy Blue." Crowley spoke the words slowly and watched the family's reactions. There were a few blank looks from the younger members of the clan, but the older ones were a different story. A few scoffed and the others blanched.

Blondie shook his head. "Would you care to elaborate?"

"Certainly." The smile he flashed was purely predatory, and the man flinched as surely as if Crowley had spat at him. "Little Boy Blue, according to the diary of Walter Alexander Bloome the second, is the pet name given in the local papers to a boy of unknown origins who was found dead at the edge of the Beldam Woods in upper state New York almost a hundred years ago. There was a rumor that the boy died in a house fire and was dropped in the woods to hide the body."

"What has that to do with anything?" Blondie was exactly the sort of person who annoyed Crowley the most: self-important and used to having the last word.

"Chester, perhaps if you'd allow Mr. Crowley the luxury of finishing his sentences and arguments we might all learn what he's trying to explain." Anita Bloome's voice was soft, but stern.

Chester threw an apologetic look in her direction and then nodded for Crowley to continue.

"Not far from the town of Beldam Woods is another town called Serenity Falls. A great deal of land in Serenity Falls was sold to a man named Blackwell early in the last century. Blackwell purchased that land from Jason and Solomon Bloome, sons of Richard Bloome. It was a very substantial sale and cemented the family's fortune.

Crowley made sure he spoke only to Chester for a moment, long enough to ensure the man grew uncomfortable.

"Before they sold the land at a substantial profit, they purchased all of that stretch from several different families of farmers. There were an unfortunate number of accidents that the families in question went through, including several drownings, at least two murders, and a small series of house fires."

Crowley smiled.

Chester swallowed nervously and nodded his head, finally understanding the gist of what the man was saying. Just to clarify for everyone else, Crowley continued speaking.

"There were rumors that the Bloomes managed to coerce a few sales to their family. Nothing that could be proved, of course, but rumors. In the long run, all that matters is that your family managed to purchase the land just in time to sell it for a very, very large profit.

"And that is where Little Boy Blue comes into the picture." Crowley stood and paced, once again making eye contact with almost every member of the family. He wanted them to understand his words.

"Around the same time that the family once again grew financially well off, a strange sickness fell on the Bloomes. If you look back over the family history, you'll see that over twenty members of the family suffered from, 'A strange wasting sickness that causes loss of teeth, blindness and hair loss, and finally death.'"

Crowley walk closer to Chester's table. "Sound familiar to you now, Chester? Sound like something that might have an impact on what's happening with the Bloome family tree?"

Chester looked away from him and nodded, properly chastised at last.

"I looked into the papers. There was no discernible connection except for the blood ties between family members. No one who married into the family died from the illness, but their children did. Distance didn't matter, and several members of the Bloome family were killed while traveling, including one Gabriella Bloome, who died while on a cruise ship."

Crowley paused for a moment to let them absorb his words. When they started to look restless, he called their attention back to him and finished.

"That's all part of your family history. It's possible you've heard all about the deaths. What you might not have heard is that several of the family members claimed they saw a young boy with, and I'm quoting here, 'blue toned skin and eyes that showed only the whites, as if he had been dead for some time, but was still approaching, still speaking.' It happened enough to make your ancestor write it down in his journals. He made the conclusion on his own, because he had a little knowledge that most of the family did not know. You see, he was with his uncle and his father when they went into the farms around Serenity Falls and committed a few atrocities to convince the locals to sell their land. He was the one who lit the farmhouse fire that killed a little boy named Lucian Hollister. And he was the one who wrote about seeing the blue boy before he finally succumbed to the odd wasting illness. The notes I found were his deathbed confession. He made a few speculations about what was happening. Among the rumors he gathered were the following: the family of Lucian Hollister was reputed to be a gathering of pagans. That the father took the last of his money and hired a witch in the Beldam Woods to curse the Bloome family, and that the ghost of Lucien Hollister was simply angry enough to hunt down and kill every member of the family that murdered him."

"Yes, we've most of us heard the stories, Mr. Crowley. But that's all they are, stories." Chester waved his hand impatiently.

"Anita Bloome asked me here to see if I could find the cause of the family problem. I've done so. Your family is currently under a curse. It only strikes one member of the family at a time and it kills until either the family is thinned to an appropriate level or something else stops it. Whatever that something else might be, I have no idea. The odds are good that the curse would have remained inactive indefinitely, but Dennis Bloome recently went up to look at colleges from what I understand, and I'd say the odds are good that he visited Beldam Woods in the process. Whatever the case, the curse has been awakened and unless it's stopped, the vast majority of blood-relations within the Bloome family will die."

Crowley crossed his arms and stared hard at Chester. It was official: the fat bastard was annoying.

"And I suppose you can stop this curse?" Chester's flabby upper lip curled into a sneer worthy of Elvis Presley.

"Yes. I can."

"And I suppose there's a cost for your services?"

"Not really, no."

"You do this out of the goodness of your heart. How Noble." The sneer was actually getting bigger.

Crowley flashed a grin and opened his mouth to comment, but before he could Anita stood up.

"Chester Martin William Bloome." Her voice was as cold as ice and the look she fired in his direction would have withered a petrified tree. "You'd do well to remember your place here. Dr. Crowley is my guest, and this is my house. You'll keep a civil tongue, young man, or you will most assuredly regret it."

Crowley coughed into his hand and moved closer to Chester. "I have more money than you, Chester. I have more money than your family. I don't need money."

"Well then, what do you need, 'Doctor' Crowley?"

Crowley smiled. "Respect, for one. And I need to be asked nicely if I'll help."

"Well, won't you please help us save our family from the big bad curse?" The pudgy man's face was quivering. His eyes were furious, but the deliberate expression of loss on his face was meant to be an insult.

Crowley smiled again. "You don't believe in ghosts, or goblins, or things that go bump in the night? Is that what the problem here is, Chester?"

"This is the twenty-first century, Mr. Crowley. Kindly grow up."

"It's Doctor Crowley to you, you pompous little shit."

"Doctor of what? Witchery?" The man was showboating, stalling and delaying in hopes that someone would come to his rescue.

Anita started to speak again and Crowley silenced her with one hand held in her direction.

"Psychology, actually. Also comparative religions, parapsychology, and a healthy side of mythology." Crowley moved closer, staring into Chester's eyes until the man could no longer stand to look at him any longer. If he wanted a display of machismo, Crowley was more than capable of beating him down.

"All of which means exactly nothing in the real world."

Crowley smiled.

"Sit there a minute, sport. Let's see about that."

He turned and walked back to Anita.

"I've done what you asked. Now, do you want me to remove the curse?"

"Yes, please, Dr. Crowley."

"You can call me Jonathan." He took a slow, deep breath. "Anita, you have to ask me. Say it out loud for me. Ask me to help you."

"Will you break the curse on my family, Jonathan?"

He smiled and nodded.

"You watching, Chester? This one's just for you, buddy. We can talk afterward, if you'd like."

Chester sneered again. He was really quite gifted in that department.

Jonathan pulled a small cloth bag from within his slacks and opened it up. Inside were several crystals of insignificant value. He took one of them and put the others away. The single crystal he squeezed between his fingers while Chester watched on. The stone was perhaps three carats in weight. It shattered into a fine dust between his fingertips and Chester blanched. Apparently the man knew enough to understand the sort of strength required to break even a low-quality stone.

Crowley muttered the words he spoke softly. They did not require volume, merely the utterance. The crushed stone blew from his hand as if hit by a powerful gust of wind and struck Chester Bloome squarely in the face.

Bloome stood up, coughing and crying out in shock. He looked at Crowley and sneered again. "That's assault! I'll see you in court you sanctimonious—" His voice cut off abruptly as he stared past Crowley and looked at a woman who failed to resemble him in any way.

Chester's eyes flew wide as he looked at her. "Mariah? What in the name of God!"

Crowley smiled. He knew exactly what Chester was seeing. Mariah turned her head to look at Chester as he spoke and opened her mouth to respond, but instead of answering him, she paled and slipped a little lower in her seat.

The creature that stood next to her was a pasty blue in color. A cherub of a boy if ever there was one, but his skin was rotting, or held that appearance, bloated and ready to sluice away at the gentlest touch. The eyes of the boy were rolled back in his head, showing only the yellowed whites.

It stepped away from Mariah, who promptly began coughing, and moved toward Chester.

Crowley continued to smile.

"What are you? What are you?" Chester shook his head and stepped back, further away from the boy-thing. In response it came closer to him, its face twisting into a parody of youthful smile for a moment before it opened its mouth. The flesh of the lip split, and a thick, dark fluid spilled down the chin.

Crowley watched it moving closer to Chester and crossed his arms. The heavyset man looked in his direction with a panic-stricken expression, his eyes showing comprehension at last. The man knew what was approaching him and did nothing to help.

Chester turned and ran, knocking aside one of his relatives and tripping over a chair in the process. He let out a scream as the blue boy leaped onto a table and then pounced at him like a stalking cat.

The creature landed on Chester's belly and squatted over him as Crowley watched. Then the vile open mouth stretched wider still until the dark fluids that ran from the ruined lips poured over the lower half of the nightmarish face, painting it a darker shade of blue. The face contorted and the dead white eyes narrowed as a black tongue as thick as a python slid from the ruined mouth and struck out at Chester's face.

Chester let out of scream that was suddenly silenced by the sick black tube that shoved into his mouth. He gagged and bucked, his eyes wide and terrified, his hands lashed out at the diminutive figure on his chest, but failed to dislodge it. He might as well have tried to push the Earth from its orbit.

Crowley watched on as the Bloome family climbed over their seats and approached Chester, looking at him with worried expressions, calling to him and asking if he were all right. Only Anita looked at Crowley then, her face unreadable, her eyes staring a challenge at him.

With a sigh, Jonathan walked over to Chester and stared at the thing on top of him. Little Boy Blue indeed. The clothing was a hundred years out of date, the face that of a young boy. He understood exactly what it was, why it looked the way it did, and what it was doing to the man.

"Chester, say hello to Little Boy Blue. Currently he's feeding on your life force. He'll do so until you're dead, unless I stop him. No one else can see him, because I wanted to make a point here. You doubted me, and you insulted me. I don't much like you. I can let you die if you like. You'll have a few weeks to get your affairs in order, because Little Boy Blue here is supposed to make you suffer. Or, if you ask me nicely, I can remove the curse from you and your family, and when I'm done you can thank me." He stepped back as Chester moaned and gagged some more, sitting up and looking in his direction with wild, panic-stricken eyes.

The black tongue that was pushed into his mouth stopped him from speaking.

Crowley smiled. "Come on now, Chester. You just have to ask. You can do that, can't you?" His eyes lit up with amusement.

Chester crawled. The curse moved like a spider, sliding over his body, wrapping its arms and legs around the man's waist and neck as it settled in. The only part of the thing that did not move was the tongue, which stayed buried in his throat, choking him. Crowley could see the faint fluttering light of Chester's life force draining through the black tongue as surely as he could see the black fluids that spilled over the flabby man's face and across his expensive shirt.

"Come on, Chester! You have to want it! You have to ask me nicely!"

The people in the room stared at Crowley, some puzzled, others horrified by his sadistic grin. He ignored all of them and stared at the man who'd acted like an ass a few moments before.

There was a modicum of immediate danger, but it was a small threat. Had Chester actually managed to force the curse away from his body, it would likely have torn him into shreds then and there to avoid being seen. Chester wasn't strong enough by half to accomplish the feat.

The man looked at Crowley and rose to his knees. He clasped his hands together and held them out in a silent plea.

Jonathan Crowley nodded his head. "That's better."

There were curses in the world that could level towns, ruin kingdoms and sink continents. In his time, Jonathan Crowley had dealt with many of them. In comparison, the demonic Little Boy Blue was barely more than a parlor trick.

He reached out with his hands and caught the silent entity in his fingers. It struggled, fought desperately, and clawed at Chester as it tried to hold on. Where Chester had failed, Crowley simply pulled with little more force than he would use on a six-year-old and lifted the thing into his arms.

On the ground, Chester groaned and coughed before finally catching a breath. He looked at Crowley, at the thing in his grasp, and then pushed himself across the ground, whimpering.

The curse immediately curled in on itself, the more distorted features of its face reverting into a childlike innocence as it became inactive. Only Chester and Crowley saw it. To everyone else, it surely looked like Crowley was pantomiming holding an infant.

"Lucien Hollister was five years old when he was murdered, Chester. Killed by your ancestors because they wanted to secure a good future for you and everyone else in your family. They probably didn't mean to kill him, but there it is."

Crowley whispered to himself, spoke words that were never meant to be heard by human ears and watched as a small boy in his arms dissolved into nothingness.

"Might want to keep that in mind if you're the sort of businessman who believes in winning at any cost. Sometimes the losers take it personally. Sometimes the winners aren't really getting everything they expected."

He turned from Chester, no longer even amused by him, and looked to Anita Bloome.

"That should be the end of it. If there are any other problems, you know the number."

"I can't thank you enough, Jonathan."

"Sure you can." He smiled tightly. "Next time, make sure Chester keeps his mouth shut." He nodded briefly at the gathered people and headed for the door.

Once outside, Crowley stared at the building he'd left and tried to sense if anything remained of the curse. There was nothing he could feel, just ghosts, and the echoes of past sins. And really, the same could be said of almost any home that held people for more than a generation.

He climbed into his car and listened as the engine fired itself into activity. The vehicle fairly purred.

"Let's get out of here. I'm about done with blue bloods for now." He yawned and leaned back a bit as the car backed away from where it had been parked and started down the long driveway.

"Hey, you think we'll see George anywhere on that road? I could use a good distraction." The car did not respond. Just to hear someone, Crowley talked. "Listen, you should have seen the loser in that house. Chester. What a name. Made George seem macho.

As he was reaching for the radio dials, his phone rang.

"This is Jonathan Crowley. How can I help you?"

The voice that answered belong to his past, but sometimes seemed to forget that fact.

"Jonathan? It's Amelia."

He swallowed the harsh comment that threatened to spill past his lips. "What can I do for you, Amelia?"

"Jonathan, it's my father." Her voice broke a bit as she spoke.

He frowned. Vernon Dunlow was a demonologist, allegedly retired.

"What did Vernon do now, Amelia?"

"Jonathan, he's dead. My daddy is dead." Her voice was so small, so very weak, and he knew that he'd go to her, try to help her. She'd always had that effect on him.

Vendetta

The rain fell in a light, annoying mist. Just enough to get you wet, but not enough to soak you. Jonathan Crowley hadn't brought an umbrella. Not that he much cared.

Despite the chilly, damp weather, there was a very large crowd at the funeral of Vernon Dunlow. Not a surprise, really, when one considered how much the man was worth. In his lifetime Dunlow had amassed a fortune worthy of kings. He'd done it slowly, methodically, and with a little help from the supernatural.

Not that long ago, Crowley reckoned, Dunlow had been a very powerful demonologist. He'd summoned the dark spirits for power, for wealth, and even to bring his dying daughter back to life. He'd screwed up on the last one. She was alive, but hardly mortal anymore.

Luckily for her, she normally behaved herself.

That was why he was standing in the rain at a funeral. Not to mourn the loss of Vernon Dunlow—though despite the demon issues he was a good enough man—but because of Amelia Dunlow. He was here to pay his respects and to check up on her.

Oh, and to get those last few books Vernon had been stupid enough to hide from him the last time he'd been to see the family.

Amelia stood near the hole in the ground where her father would soon be interred. She was, without doubt, the most beautiful woman Crowley had ever seen. Hardly a challenge under the circumstances. She'd had a little help as it were.

Every man in the area and a few of the women as well would have probably loved to be with her in a sexual relationship. Some would have gleefully sold their souls. Most of them would never get the chance.

The man standing beside her on the other hand, Mike Blake, was probably with her regularly. Crowley was a little surprised to see Blake at her side, especially at the funeral. The last time he'd seen the man he was still warring over whether he would go to be with Amelia or sit in his living room and get numbingly drunk. Alcoholics almost always face that sort of decision. His estimation of the man went up a notch. He'd felt absolutely certain that Blake would fall back into the bottle.

Amelia was dressed in black; a veil covered part of her face and her long, elegant form leaned against Mike. He was also in black, a suit that cost more than he'd been making a year when he met Amelia. Blake held an umbrella over Amelia, defending her from the rain that drizzled down and wetted the side of his face and the growing bald spot on the top of his head. There were no other mourners standing close to the two of them. There was no other family to consider. Amelia was alone in the world, except for Blake.

Crowley cast his eyes over the crowd. Most of them were obvious business associates of Vernon Dunlow. A few of them were likely close friends of the family. The Dunlows had a lot of friends. They were honest people and generous with their wealth. It hadn't been all that long ago that Fortune Magazine had done an article on the Dunlow family and their policies concerning benefits for their employees. Despite the climate of looking out for the top dollar and cutting benefits that dominated corporate America, the Dunlows had kept up with good retirement packages, excellent health benefits, and even stock option bonuses for their staff.

They had remarkably little turnover in their ten thousand plus employees, which came as no surprise.

Every person there would likely miss Vernon Dunlow as the years passed; even the ones who'd never really known him very well. That was a fine testament to the man's memory.

Crowley waited until the mourners began cycling in front of the lowered coffin before he started moving forward. Amelia hadn't seen him yet. Neither had Blake. He'd have bet money neither of them was actually expecting him, either. Jonathan Crowley was not known for making social visits.

Amelia listened to the condolences of the people in front of him and nodded her head, answering each well-wisher automatically. Mike did the same, but he held himself like a man trying to avoid getting confrontational. That much hadn't changed. He was desperate to keep Amelia safe at all times. *Good,* Crowley mused. *That's good. The more he wants her safe, the easier it is for me to ignore her existence.*

The procession moved with slow, steady speed. Crowley looked at the people ahead of him and spotted one who seemed familiar. He was a stocky man, not fat, but heavyset, with a silvery crew cut and a black suit that was perfectly tailored to fit him. He was exactly the sort of man who looked like he'd be comfortable knocking back cheap beer at a local bar or sipping champagne with royalty. Crowley recognized him immediately and felt the smile try to grow on his face. He forced the expression back. There'd be time enough for that later.

Mike saw him first. The man's eyes flew wide for a moment and then lowered to half-mast, as if he were expecting trouble. Considering how well they'd gotten along previously, Crowley wasn't shocked by that. Then again, something about Blake pissed Crowley off and always had.

Amelia spotted him and despite the circumstances, he saw the excitement in her eyes. She lowered her head to hide the expression and Crowley took two more steps forward.

The gray-haired man stopped before the two mourners and offered his condolences. Mike shook his hand and thanked him for showing up. He spoke to the man with respect and Crowley bit his tongue to stop from making a scene. He had no intention of causing problems at the funeral.

There would be time for dealing with the man later, after the services.

Amelia saw the man and spoke more formally. She understood just how dangerous the stranger was, and how powerful his influence could be. That made her the exception, not the rule.

Albert Miles, for his part, was the very image of kindness. That was his way. He spoke softly and genuinely. Crowley had no doubt in his mind that every word the man spoke was completely sincere.

Another few paces forward and it was his turn to say hello.

Mike managed a weak smile. It was probably the best he could offer.

"Mike. I'm sorry for your loss."

"Thank you, Jonathan. It's good of you to come. I know Amelia appreciates it."

"The least I could do, I'm sure. Vernon was a good man."

"Yes, he was. He'll be missed." Oh, he could tell how much Mike Blake disliked him, and all that knowledge did was increase his amusement.

Instead of saying anything else, he nodded again and moved over to say hello to Amelia. Up close her beauty was even more evident. Eyes that could capture a man's soul, lips that could, he felt certain, drive a man to extreme acts with only a few whispered words. She was physical perfection from head to toe, not a single flaw to be found.

"Hello, Amelia. I'm sorry."

Amelia barely looked at him. "We'll talk later, if that's okay, Jonathan." Her lips trembled, her shoulders hitched slightly.

"Of course. I'll see you in a little while."

He took her hands in his and held them for the briefest moment; just long enough to feel her fingers twitch, to hear her intake of breath, and then he moved on.

The funeral was ending, so he moved toward the parking lot and his car.

A quick glimpse showed him that Albert Miles was heading for his own vehicle, a glossy black Rolls Royce.

He quickened his pace and stepped closer to the man, placing a hand on his shoulder.

"I remember you." The words were purred into Miles' ear. "I remember you very well, indeed."

Most people, Crowley knew from experience, would prefer not to be remembered by him. It was almost always an indication of bad things to come.

Albert Miles turned toward him and smiled as pleasantly as if he were seeing an old friend. "Mister Crowley. What a delightful surprise."

"Hasn't been long enough in my book, Mr. Miles, but then, I believe we have unfinished business between us."

"Really? What sort of business?"

"Something to do with you killing Serenity Falls."

"Nonsense, my good man. The town is still there, isn't it? I visited it only a few weeks ago."

"I'm sure you did." Crowley smiled. Ten feet away from him, one of the mourners looking in their direction suddenly remembered that he had better things to do and scrambled for his car keys.

"Have you been back there, to Serenity Falls, Mr. Crowley? I think they're making delightful progress. You'd barely be able to tell there was ever a disaster in the town."

"Let's keep it that way, Mr. Miles. I think the people there have suffered enough."

"Oh, really! I hardly have the time to consider the past anymore, Mr. Crowley. I have other matters to attend to."

Crowley's smile grew larger still, wide enough now to make his jaws ache.

Miles looked at him with eyes almost the same color as his hair and smiled back, a cheerful, familiar expression. He would, Crowley suspected, have used the exact same smile if he were telling grandchildren tales of Santa Claus, or if he were in the process of cutting a bound man into shreds of raw meat.

"Now is not the time to discuss what you have in mind for other people and places, Mr. Miles. But rest assured, we will be discussing matters in the near future."

Miles laughed politely. "Is this the point where I should give you another distraction, a chance for me to escape from your attention for a time?" His voice was rich and jovial.

"Now is the time for you to put your affairs in order, Mr. Miles. I still haven't quite forgiven you for what you did."

"Oh, Mr. Crowley, I'd be disappointed if you had."

The man looked at his watch and tsked. "I'm afraid we will have to have this discussion another time. I have a plane to catch." He put his hand out for shaking and Crowley gripped it firmly. There was a piece of paper there, folded exactly twice and no larger than an index card. "I've a gift for you, Mr. Crowley. I believe you've been looking for the man on that paper for a very long time."

"Why would you give me a gift, Mr. Miles?"

"I can appreciate your reasons for looking, Mr. Crowley. I lost a wife, too, as you might well recall."

Crowley felt his stomach fall away into an abyss.

"What did you say?" His voice was barely a whisper.

"I said it was lovely seeing you again, Mr. Crowley. I look forward to having a proper chat sometime soon." There was mischief in his eyes. "Don't worry. I won't warn him that you're coming. That would ruin the fun. Besides, I no longer have any need for associating with that particular individual. He's become...a hindrance, if you will."

Crowley stood perfectly still as Albert Miles climbed into the Silver Cloud. He was still standing there five minutes later when the vehicle drove out of sight.

Finally, he looked at the paper as Amelia and Mike were escorted to the limousine that would drive them back to her home.

The writing was neat and precise. A single name and address to go with it were all that were written on the paper.

Really, they were all that was needed. Crowley folded the paper and slipped it into his jacket pocket.

He tried to ignore the fact that his hands were trembling with suppressed rage.

He still had to deal with Amelia and the books her father had hidden away.

The rooms of the Dunlow mansion were filled with strangers, people that meant nothing at all to Amelia. Still, it was her place to be with them; to listen to their endless babbling about how well remembered her father was. She had always known that someday he would pass, but she'd never thought he would go so suddenly.

Vernon Dunlow had always been the picture of vitality, strong and handsome even as he grew older. He had a checkup every six months and always came back with a clean bill of health. The heart attack came as a complete surprise to everyone who knew him, including the family physician.

Thinking about him made her eyes sting with unshed tears. She had been raised to understand that the time and place for mourning was when you were alone. No one was meant to share your sorrow but the people closest to you. Mike understood that, too. That was why he was leaving her in peace. He knew she'd come to him when she was ready.

The front door opened again and Jonathan Crowley walked into the room, his dark suit and overcoat tastefully subdued, his long face and short brown hair were as unremarkable as ever; almost nondescript, really. He could blend in with a crowd in most places without even trying.

Still, he walked like a monarch entering his palace, as if the world belonged to him and everything he saw was his. His face was set and calm, but his eyes, oh, how his eyes burned, even behind the rimless glasses he wore to hide them away. Without even trying to sense his emotions, she could feel the fury within him, a sensation that was only shocking because it hadn't been there half an hour ago.

He scanned the room quickly and then headed directly for her.

There were no pleasantries. There were never any pleasantries when Jonathan came around. They weren't his thing. Truth be told, he wasn't a very pleasant man. Still, he made her heart beat increase.

He had that effect on everyone, though seldom for the same reasons.

"Hello, Jonathan." She spoke softly, as if afraid to anger him.

"I'm sorry, Amelia. I really am."

"That means a lot." She looked around for a moment and then started walking toward her father's office. She knew without bothering to look that he would follow her. A moment later she was leaning against her father's desk and Crowley was closing the door.

"You know why I'm here, right?"

"Of course. You want the books." She tried not to let her disappointment show.

"I can get the books any time. I want to see how you're holding up." The rage she'd seen in his face was gone, replaced by concern, nothing more and nothing less.

Without any intention of doing anything of the sort, Amelia broke into tears and reached out, her hands going around his chest as she practically fell into him.

She cried so hard she could barely take in a breath, and Crowley put his arms around her, holding her tightly. She could feel the concern that he had for her, but without even trying to read his emotions, she could also feel the rage inside him, a furnace that burned far too hot with the power to scar and destroy.

He held her, and unlike most of the men she knew, he never made a move. He was one of the few men in the world she could trust to behave himself, much as she might have wished a few times in the past that he weren't.

Hot tears scalded her face as they ran down her skin and soaked into his jacket. She wanted to apologize because she knew exactly how much he hated getting dirty, but there were no words left in her. She'd been accepting the platitudes of strangers and the condolences of people who meant nothing to her for the last week, and the single person she never expected to hear from was standing in front of her and offering silent comfort.

Finally, when the crying jag came to an end, leaving her worn out and hollow, Crowley leaned forward slightly and kissed her once on the top of her head.

"Why are you so angry today, Jonathan?"

"Nothing to worry yourself about." He stared hard at her, and she knew he was assessing how well her wards were working. There'd been a time, not that long ago, really, when she couldn't have kept the wards in place without his help. Jonathan Crowley had been remarkably kind to her over the years, kinder than she would have expected from a man who hunted and destroyed almost anything he encountered that fell outside of the mundane.

"I haven't felt this sort of anger off of you since..." She cut herself short. There had been times in the past when Jonathan had not been himself, when he was close to death, and she'd been the one to help him through those times. Whether he'd wanted the help or not.

"Since the asylum?" his voice was calm, almost amused, but she felt the increase in his anger as easily as most people could see.

Amelia looked away from him as guilt assaulted her. She knew in her heart that he hadn't forgiven her for what happened back then.

"I have to go, Amelia. I have things to take care of."

"Stay for a few days, Jonathan." She hated how needy she sounded.

"I can't." That was all he had to say about the subject. There was no discussing the matter and she knew better than to try.

Amelia cried again, and he held her through it, though she could feel his growing impatience.

Twenty minutes later he'd gathered the four volumes her father had left behind and headed for the door. His anger lingered in the room long after the scent of his cologne had faded away.

Jonathan Crowley drove up Interstate 95 at close to 100 miles per hour, shifting around the cars that moved too slowly for his satisfaction. The car's tires hummed, and the engine purred. There were a few advantages to having his abilities and one of them was a car that repaired itself and always stayed in perfect running condition.

His mind wasn't on the road. Every adjustment he made may as well have been set by an autopilot.

His mind was reeling back through the years, remembering things he'd thought to have put behind him once and for all.

Once upon a time, longer back than he wanted to recall, he'd been happy. Truly happy. It hadn't lasted. Couldn't have, really. Not in hindsight.

He'd had a wife and children. They were gone, murdered, killed before his very eyes, but only after they'd been tortured savagely.

He'd put them to rest in his mind, knowing that they were well beyond his ability to bring back into his life, but the thing that had killed them? Well, that was a different story entirely.

Being the Hunter kept him busy, but that had never stopped him from looking when he could, searching for the unclean thing that had stolen them from him. The problem was it knew how to hide itself away.

Nearly forty years, and if he were to be truthful with himself, he'd never recovered from the loss. Never forgotten the sounds of Jeremy and Wendy screaming, or the sobs of Theresa as she looked on her mother's ruined remains. Or the muted, desperate cries of…

Elizabeth, Oh Lord, how I miss you…

…his wife dying after the sick fuck had tortured her beyond all repair.

Try as he might to forget all of them, and all of the joy of their lives and the sorrow of their deaths, they were there, lingering in the back of his mind constantly.

"Enough of this," he grunted the words under his breath as he wove past another car that may as well have been standing still.

Crowley fiddled with the car's radio, searching for a station that had tolerable music. If he heard one more fifteen-year-old girl singing about heartbreak, he was going to have to hurt someone.

Pausing for a moment, he found a station playing bubblegum music instead, and sure enough, a teenaged girl was singing about how hard it was to be in love. He left it to play as the teen crooned and wailed on about her tragedies.

He was in the mood to hurt someone, after all. And he knew just who he was planning to hurt.

Crowley's lips pulled back into the smile he'd been suppressing earlier.

"Robert Anthony Workham...What's that old saying? 'When I get through with you, there won't be anything left.'"

The tires kept humming and the cars kept getting passed. Jonathan Crowley thought long and hard about the things he intended to do once he found Robert Workham. None of them would be gentle.

Bob Workham settled back at his office desk and looked out the window. A long, long ways off, the cars drove and the people moved and lived their lives. He smiled at the thought. There had been a time when he would have been raging, desperate to destroy all of them. It was a part of his nature. Being a demon meant thriving on destruction and corruption.

That was then. These days he'd come to a sort of peace with his unusual position. There were very few demons, no matter how powerful, who managed to walk the earth for long. He'd learned new tricks along the way and sacrificed a good portion of his power to arrange it, but the loss of his energies had been well worth it.

There were costs, of course. Bargains had been made, and some of them had already come due. Still, all of it was well worth the price, especially when he considered what he had gained with his freedom.

He was a family man now. The thought of his wife, his children, made him smile.

The large desk in his office was almost Spartan, but it did have a portrait of his wife, Colleen and his children, Amy, Bob Jr., and Steven set in a place of honor.

Colleen was a beauty, as many a man had told him. She was also one of the sharpest women he'd ever met. Before he'd run across her, he had felt certain he was destined to be alone. All he had to do was think about his previous wife—his previous life, really—and he could see the differences.

He tried to shake off the memory of how that relationship had ended. Sometimes, late at night when he was looking back on his time among the humans, he wished he could go back and change a few of his actions.

The girl in Boston had deserved better than she got.

Still it was in the past now; there was nothing to be done about it.

He sighed and picked up the phone. Enough of fond memories. One last bit of work to do and then he could see about heading away from the office.

The phone rang three times before somebody answered. The familiar voice sounded harried, which was exactly what he liked to hear from his subordinates.

"Alex, this is Bob. I wanted to know how far you've gotten with locating Albert Miles for me."

"Nowhere, Bob. I've gotten nowhere at all." Alex managed to sound both harried and apologetic.

"That's not acceptable. Miles and I have some unfinished business. I need to attend to it." He didn't bother waiting for excuses, but disconnected the call instead.

A nervous storm washed through his insides. The feeling wasn't one he was familiar with, even after two lifetimes as a human being. It was called fear, and he was far more used to causing it than suffering from it.

For all the advantages of being in human form, the emotions still got to him, and this one, this fear, was the worst of them all.

It wasn't the money. The money was good. He had arranged that little bonus a long time ago, not long after he'd managed to steal the body of the fool who'd summoned him. Inevitably, the self-proclaimed demonologists made mistakes, from making payments too late to simple errors in the wards they created, all of them screwed up sooner or later. Well, most of them. There were a few who were cautious enough to survive for a long time. All it had taken was another fool willing to bargain away his soul for a better life and he'd been on his way to wealth and success, along with the body of the man who'd summoned him in the first place.

So, no, money wasn't an issue.

It was a matter of security. Over the last few decades he'd come to understand that human life was a delicate thing, easily broken and stolen away.

He'd learned that for himself when he'd run across the Hunter while unprepared for trouble. He'd learned it again after the troubles with his first wife and their child together. That had been a mess, and one he didn't like to think about.

He'd been foolish back then, almost begging to get caught and sent back to what the humans called Hell…as if they could even begin to understand what was waiting beyond the veil that separated worlds.

Almost anything was preferable to heading back to that location, even making bargains with humans like Albert Miles.

He clenched his fists unconsciously at the thought of the man. Miles had something he needed, and in return, the man demanded power.

Albert Miles was a sorcerer, and quite a good one, apparently. He'd managed to keep Bob hidden from discovery for a long, long time, requesting only an occasional sacrifice or favor in return. He had one more payment to go before he would be done with the man, and now, like one of the demonologists he used to play games with when they made their bargains, payment was due.

Only this time it was Bob who owed and he was desperate to make restitution before it was too late.

Therefore, he had to deal with Miles. Either by coming to an arrangement, or by having the man destroyed. He preferred coming to an arrangement, because from everything he'd heard, Albert Miles was not exactly a pushover.

It was almost six in the evening, and he'd done enough for one day. The office would be here in the morning and so would the troubles that came with it. In the meantime, Bob Jr. had a game tonight and he intended to be there. He'd never hear the end of it if he missed another game.

He looked at his watch and realized he had just enough time to get there if he left immediately.

When the phone rang again, he ignored it. Business could wait for business hours.

Amelia lay next to Mike on the bed, unable to sleep, unable to even rest comfortably. It wasn't a very common feeling for her. She usually had little trouble with the notion of getting sleep. The innocent seldom do.

Now, however, she was worried about Jonathan Crowley. He was so very, very furious and she hadn't felt rage like that coming off of him in decades, really. He was very good at leaving his anger at a slow, deadly burn as opposed to the conflagration she'd felt coming off of him in waves.

Normally she could shelter her mind from the emotions of others, but Jonathan was an exception. He was the one who'd taught her to protect herself, after all. The only time she got nothing from him was when he decided to block her abilities and shield himself from her probing mind. She shouldn't have had any issues with blocking the feelings coming from him, and she suspected in the long run it was because she *wanted* to know what he was thinking and feeling.

A bad habit, that. It was best to forget that the man existed. Knowing Jonathan Crowley could be listed as an occupational hazard. Caring for him could be called having a death wish.

Moving with a grace that would have shamed a cat, Amelia slid off the bed and left Mike where he was, deep in a dream. For once, it seemed like a good dream and not more recollections of his life in Serenity Falls.

She slipped on a robe and moved down the stairs to her father's office and sat in the luxurious leather throne he called an office chair.

A quick flash of pain went through her at the thought of her father. After a week she still had trouble believing he was dead. He had been such a vital part of her life, her world, that the idea of him being gone forever was a new misery, one she had never prepared herself for. Throughout her life, her father had been the one constant and now she was stuck wondering what she would do with herself.

Oh, the business would keep her busy, but it wouldn't make up for the loss of the man who'd raised her.

She opened the drawers of his desk, one at a time, and studied the contents. There were two drawers she wasn't supposed to open, but whatever secrets he wanted kept from her were now Amelia's to deal with.

That was the way it had to be. There could be no more secrets between them, even if he wanted them kept from her for all time.

One of the drawers held several address books. She pulled them out and scanned the pages for a moment before putting them back.

The other drawer held books of a different sort. The type that Jonathan Crowley would have interest in. She opened the first and looked at the words. They made no sense to her, not that she was surprised by that. Books like the ones her father had used in his earlier years were notorious for being written in code or, according to Jonathan, sometimes just couldn't be read by people who didn't have the intent to use them. Amelia had no intent to do anything with them but give them to Jonathan when he came back from wherever he'd gone. It looked to be a bumper crop for unholy books in her household, despite the promises her father had made years earlier.

That line of thought brought her back to where she'd been when she was lying in bed and wishing for sleep.

She was worried about Jonathan. Silly, of course, because she knew he could heal from anything given enough time, but the worry remained just the same.

She looked through the books her father had hidden away, just to keep herself distracted. The second set of books were useless, so she tried the first batch again, sorting through each one, looking at names and numbers that meant nothing to her. From time to time her father's precise handwriting had jotted notes next to certain names. Most of them were simple notes referencing business. A few were doodles that made clear he could have done without the individuals in his life.

One of the simple notes, concise and clear, said "Watch out for him. Deadlier than he looks." The name meant nothing to her, but she made note of it. As she progressed through the pages there were a few more along those lines and she made a list of the names as she came across them. It was best to know whom she might be dealing with in the long run.

She came to the name Robert Workham and read the note her father had written. She read it again, just to be sure what she'd read was correct.

The words were direct, even if they were in the form of a question: Killed Crowley's Family?

Amelia stared at the simple phrase for a long time, barely able to breathe.

Workham had killed Jonathan's family? Might have killed them? And her father had known?

The notion terrified her.

Not because she feared that Jonathan would be wounded by her father's knowledge, but because she knew that if he wanted it badly enough, Jonathan Crowley could find her father's spirit wherever it might be and make him suffer for not informing him. She wasn't sure how he would do it; merely that he was perfectly capable of it.

Amelia closed the books and looked at the phone.

Loyalty to her father meant not telling Jonathan.

Loyalty to Jonathan meant he'd want to know the truth. He needed to know the truth, even if it was only a possibility and not a certainty.

Jonathan Crowley had been hunting for a long time, and he was not the sort to forgive or to forget a slight. He was just possibly the scariest man she'd ever met in her entire life, and Amelia had met a lot of scary men in her time.

Midnight had come and gone and Jonathan Crowley sat in a diner and sipped at coffee. The brew had been sitting around for too long and grown dark and bitter. It suited his mood so he didn't demand a fresh pot.

The rains from earlier had changed, sliding into snow and a cold wind. He wasn't dressed for the cold, but he didn't much care. He was almost where he wanted to be. Almost at the home of Robert Workham.

He was also tired, close to exhaustion. He didn't think it would be wise to deal with Workham until he'd had a chance to rest. Unfortunately, rest meant a chance to dream and to remember when his life had been closer to complete.

That, he knew from experience, wasn't always a good thing.

Better to forget, really. Better to wish it had never happened. Easier, too.

Crowley finished his coffee and stood up, heading for the door, the money to pay his check already in his hand by the time he reached the cashier.

The woman who took his money was short, portly, and had the most amazing hair he'd seen in ages. A thick, braided ponytail ran past her rear end and almost to her knees. He hated to even think about what it must take to wash the stuff.

She smiled pleasantly and told him to have a nice night. He managed a smile in return and walked outside just as his phone rang.

The cell phone only rang when someone was calling on him for help. He knew that, but still he almost resisted answering. He didn't want to save another idiot who'd summoned the wrong sort of thing, or hunt down another creature that shouldn't have even existed. He wanted to hunt down and kill one particular beast, and he was already planning to take care of that one; slowly, with deliberate and meticulous detail.

He sighed and answered the phone. "Crowley. What?"

"Mr. Crowley?" The voice was young and nervous, a teenager, maybe, or a preteen. It was hard to say for sure because the connection sucked rotten eggs.

"Yes?" He was trying to be patient. It wasn't working very well.

"Hi. Umm. You said I should call you if there was ever anything weird going on. Do you remember?"

Crowley closed his eyes and counted to ten as slowly as he could. "Well, I might, but first I need to have a name. A little something to remind me."

"Oh." There was nervous laughter on the other end of the line. "It's me, Tim Daniels."

Crowley frowned. *Daniels, Daniels…Ah, yes.* He hadn't heard from Tim Daniels in at least four years, not since he'd been murdered.

"Tim, are you aware that you're dead?"

"Well, yeah, but it's my mom, see. She's got a thing in her house and it won't leave her alone."

Crowley pinched his fingers against the bridge of his nose and pushed his frameless glasses higher up his face. "Tim, how did you even get this number?"

"You gave it to me."

"Yes, I did," he was trying to be calm. It was becoming more and more of a challenge. Still the kid was only ten when he died. "But Tim, I didn't expect you to call me from the other side of the grave, if you see what I'm getting at."

"Oh." He could almost hear the kid shrugging. "Well, I can't help that part. I just remembered you said to call you and there's no one else I can ask for help."

"Kid, nothing personal, but technically you can't even ask *me*. There are rules to this sort of thing, and I don't usually help dead people out. Somebody out there might, but it isn't me."

"But, my mom…"

Crowley shook his head, gritted his teeth and continued working on being patient. Yeah, it still wasn't going all that well. "Tim, you're not getting it, I meant what I said. There are rules I have to follow. I can't help you. You're dead. Deceased. I attended your funeral."

"I know. I saw you."

Crowley nodded his head as if the kid was watching. He'd felt Tim's presence, but dealing with ghosts wasn't really what he did. Not unless they'd become a threat to somebody living.

"Tim, pay attention. I can't do anything to help you, because the rules won't let me. I don't help the dead, I help the living."

"Well who made up the rules?" The kid sounded like he was on the verge of tears.

"I can't say."

"You don't know?"

"No, I can't say. There's a difference." Dumb as a stump this one was.

"Then who do I call?"

Ghostbusters? "I don't know. It's not really the sort of thing you can find in the Yellow Pages, Tim."

"But my mom's alive, Mr. Crowley."

He sighed. It was going to be one of those conversations. "Yes, I get that, Tim. I do. But I can't take a call for help from you. If your mom called me, I could come help her, see, but not from you."

"Why not?"

Sweet Jesus. "Because you're fucking dead! I don't help the dead!" he'd tried to be patient, but there were limits. A couple of teenagers who were out far too late looked in his direction, startled by the comment. He ignored them, much as he would have preferred to slap them around on general principle.

The connection broke up for a moment and Crowley started to hope that the call was done with.

"Well. If I find somebody to ask you, can you help her?"

"Yes. I can help then. Just have them call me."

"So can you come look at her house now, and maybe get a head start?"

"I'm sort of busy, Tim. I have a demon to kill."

"Please? Come on, I'll find somebody, honest." Desperate ghosts, like his life wasn't crappy enough.

"Tim, if you find someone alive to call me and ask, I'll get there as soon as I can. But right now I have a little unfinished business to take care of, and unless I hear from somebody living, it's going to take precedence."

"I thought you were supposed to be the good guy, Mr. Crowley." The voice was low and disappointed. Crowley felt like he'd just stolen Christmas from an orphanage.

"I am, Tim, but I still have to follow the rules."

"Well, they're stupid rules!" Ah, there it was, the anger. The dead had a tendency to get extremely bitchy; at least those that didn't move on to the great beyond, or whatever the hell lay in wait for them after their lives ended.

"Yes, Tim, they are. But I don't make them, I just follow them." Regret. Was that regret in his voice? Yes, because in the long run he'd failed the kid when he was alive and now he was in the process of failing him again.

"I trusted you, Mr. Crowley. I trusted you and you let me die. You owe me." Deeper anger now, and that whining quality that Crowley hated. He didn't care if it was a kid, a dead kid, or a grown up, he hated whining.

"It doesn't work that way, sweet pea. I do what I can, and then I leave. I don't owe you a damned thing."

"Wait! I'm sorry! Sometimes, sometimes my head gets all fuzzy."

Yeah, well, getting torn into shreds will do that to a growing boy. "Look, Tim…" *Shit.* He just wanted to make the kid understand. *I'm going to do it, aren't I?* "Give me your damned address again, okay, kid? I'll see what I can do."

"Thank you, Mr. Crowley! Thank you so much!" Crowley nodded once again, as if the kid could possibly see him, and wrote down the address.

"Look for someone to ask for help, Tim. I mean it. I can't do much without that, okay?"

"I will! I promise! I will!"

Crowley disconnected the call and sighed. The good news was the address was in a neighboring town, not far from where he was headed. The bad news was nothing sucked as much as walking into what was most likely a trap.

Crowley climbed into his car and cranked the heat. The air was getting colder, and he didn't much feel like shivering all the way to Bolingbrook, Illinois.

Bob Workham lay in bed and looked at Colleen. Sleep took the stress from her day and eased the years from her face. She'd been a beauty when they met at nineteen, and she was even lovelier now.

He didn't dare touch her, because she was a light sleeper. He just admired her, amazed as always by everything she did.

Being mortal was so much better than being a demon. He could do without the abilities he'd given up, without the power to bend steel in his hands. They were nothing next to the emotions that had taken the place of most of his abilities. Most, because he wasn't foolish enough to give up all of his powers. He never trusted that the people around him were as human as they appeared, or as innocent as the children he'd helped raise.

It didn't take a demon to kill another human being, or to savage the flesh of a child for sexual pleasure. He knew that all too well, and he had done both in his time.

Workham looked away from Colleen as the sexual desires started again. Demons didn't make love, or gently caress flesh. They bit and tore and violated the objects of their desire. Though he had never touched Colleen in those ways, the urges were still there. He didn't dare look at her now, when his memories of the past brought those darker desires closer to the surface.

He remembered the screams, the blood, the sweet scent of fear and death and try though he might to push them away, he knew it was too late.

Bob climbed carefully from his bed as his skin tried to tighten. He bit down hard on the inside of his mouth until he could feel the hot sting of broken flesh and the blood flowed freely into his mouth. Even that was not enough, not this time.

He didn't bother getting dressed, but left the room and the house as quickly as he could instead, feeling the changes that shifted muscles and bones, which threatened his family.

Dark urges, indeed.

Chicago was a very large town, and that was why he chose it. An occasional unusual death was hardly even newsworthy these days, especially if he was wise enough not to leave any evidence.

The air outside his home was freezing cold and thick snow fell from the heavens, burying the neighborhood in a caul of white.

Thick plumes of steam rushed past his lips as he moved forward, letting the change happen. Agony seared through him, but it was nothing compared to the eternities he'd spent in Hell before escaping once and for all.

His skin thickened, his muscles grew, his joints ripped themselves out of shape and rearranged into new positions that had nothing to do with the natural order. His vision changed and the darkness that had surrounded him was made as clear as the brightest day.

Despite his desires to be truly, completely human, Bob smiled. It felt good to cut loose now and then, to be true to his nature and to go out on a proper hunt.

He could smell them all around him, the weak human forms that lay sleeping or copulating in the houses nearby. Much as he wanted to tear into them, all of them, he forced himself to move on. It wouldn't do to bring unwanted attention to his life, his family.

He ran twenty blocks before he finally let himself start hunting. Twenty blocks took him to the part of Chicago that very few people wanted to call home.

The needs were powerful in him and he barely took the time to find a decent target for his lust.

The girl was young and pretty, a whore to be certain, but not completely ruined yet by her career choices. The man she was with was likely her pimp.

Two swings of his clawed hands and the man fell backward screaming, his face crosshatched with lines of blood deep enough to show bone.

The girl barely had a chance to react before he was on her, tearing away clothes and then flesh as he drank deeply of her blood and then feasted on her life essence.

He left the man where he fell, but took the girl with him, moving in shadows and skillfully peeling the meat from her bones.

Her skeleton stayed with him until he reached Evanston and dropped the bloodied bones into Lake Michigan. After that, he grabbed handfuls of snow and scrubbed her remains from his thick hide until he was certain he was properly cleaned. Then, sated, he moved back toward his home, his family, waiting until he was inside the residence to let himself change back into human form.

He was quiet as he moved through the house, checking on each of his children before he moved back into the room. By then his body temperature was back to normal, his skin no longer freezing cold.

Bob slipped into his bed and once again stared at Colleen's sleeping form. He pushed away the remnants of his demonic urges and satisfied himself with the image of the woman he loved.

Humanity was a strange creation in the universe and he was so much better for becoming a part of it.

But he could not sleep. Notions of how delicate the human life was haunted him long into the night and lingered even as the sun rose.

I can't call him. He'll be so angry.

Amelia stood under the water of her shower and shivered at the thought. There were very few things that scared her as much as Jonathan Crowley when he was angered, and he would be furious if he found out. *No,* she corrected herself, *when he finds out.*

There are advantages to being wealthy and one of them is the ability to get knowledge on anyone you want, provided you can pay for it. Amelia paid dearly for every bit of the information and never hesitated.

The darkest hours of the morning had seen to gathering the knowledge she wanted about Robert Workham. He'd done an admirable job of creating a human identity, but it wasn't good enough to hide from close scrutiny.

The investigators had been very good at finding out what they needed to. For one thing, the man's social security card was accurate, but didn't belong to him. It belonged to one Robert Corin who lived in New England. Corin had no job, no current address, not even a receipt from any of his credit cards, though they were still considered active. Robert Corin had not been seen by anyone in close to fifteen years. The man had one surviving son and one daughter, but aside from that he may as well have never existed.

The only thing they had in common was their shared Social Security Number. The pictures she'd paid for included three grainy shots of Corin and an even dozen of Robert Workham. They were different heights, different ages and even different in their builds. Corin had been broad and muscular. Workham was taller, leaner, with darker hair and a slight paunch.

Ah, but their eyes were the same. Striking, dark green eyes that managed to be looking away from the camera in every single shot.

Had she seen the two men next to each other, she would have thought them different men. Knowing what she did about demons, she had no doubt they were one and the same.

Thinking back, she couldn't remember when Jonathan had last been in Boston. She couldn't recall a single time when he'd mentioned the town, though she had no doubt he'd managed to get there on a few occasions.

The name Corin seemed familiar, but not for any reason she could identify. When she'd looked through her father's lists of addresses there had been mention of a woman with the same last name, but the only note he'd left with her contact information was that she was deceased.

Robert Corin was a ghost, long since vanished from the world. Robert Workham was alive and well and living in Chicago. He was also married with three children. She didn't want to imagine what Jonathan would do with that information. She didn't like to think about how he would react to knowing that the thing that had killed his wife and family was not only alive, but raising his own children. Two of the pictures showed Workham with his family, a beautiful redheaded woman and three youngsters, who had their mother's features and their father's dark hair.

I have to tell him.

Amelia stepped out of the shower and shivered. The thought of calling him, letting him know that she'd found the man who had probably killed his family…it wasn't a happy notion.

She thought about Crowley as she dressed, trying to decide whether or not to call him, to let him know what she had discovered.

In the end there was never really any doubt about what she would do. She had to tell him, because not telling him would be far too dangerous.

She walked into the bedroom and sat on the bed. Mike was already out of the house, off on business. He knew what had to be done and insisted on her resting for a few more days before the time came to assume her mantle as the owner of the company.

Amelia picked up the phone and considered very, very carefully dialing the numbers she knew by heart.

Her fingers struck the numbered keys before she could chicken out, and she set the receiver against her head and waited for an answer.

There were few things in Erica's life that she longed for. Her family was comfortable, her parents spoiled her rotten—a fact that she knew and tried not to take advantage of—and she had good health and plenty of people she could call friends.

What she did not have was peace.

She climbed out of her bed and yawned, stretching her body to ease the tensions that sleep had brought into her form. As far as she was concerned, fourteen-year-old girls shouldn't have issues with tension, but she managed to get them anyway.

She'd had nightmares off and on for years now, ever since her best friend growing up was murdered. She didn't remember all of the details, didn't want to remember them, but she'd been there when Tim Daniels was torn apart, and she'd been lucky enough to escape the same fate. Since then, nightmares. Not every night, thank God, but often enough to ruin her sleep about half the time. Medications didn't help, psychotherapy only did so much, and even trying prayers every night seemed to fail her.

Sometimes when she saw him in her dreams he was nice, but mostly he was angry and screaming or even crying for her to help him.

Last night's dream had been a doozy; bad enough to wake her up a few times with her hands clutching the pillow and pressing it to her face to stifle any possible screams. Somewhere along the way she'd learned to use the pillow as a muffler in her sleep. If nothing else, at least it kept her parents from freaking out. Nothing said it was time for another intense round with the local shrink like a good case of the night terrors.

Last night Tim had come to her and told her that his mother was dying, being killed by something that looked like him and pretended to be him. He told her he needed her to call Jonathan Crowley—and she remembered Crowley, because he scared the hell out of her—and that if she did, he'd never give her another nightmare.

Just to make his point, Tim started biting her in her dreams, his teeth attacking her in places that no boy had been allowed to touch! She woke up in a fit of shakes and stayed awake for at least twenty minutes.

Then she went to sleep and had the same nightmare again. If she had to guess, her dear dead friend had attacked her something like fifteen times before he was done passing on his message.

And now she'd spent another night being tormented by her dead friend's memories. Only these days it seemed he wanted to be a pervert.

Tim had been like a brother to her. The idea that he would actually haunt her was stupid. The last shrink had told her she was experiencing "Displaced anxieties pertaining to the death of your friend." That worked as well as anything else when it came to explanations. In other words, it meant absolutely nothing, except that a ghost wasn't haunting her. And really, that was good enough for her.

After her brief pause for self-mental diagnosis, Erica stood up and headed for the bathroom down the hall from her personal domain. She shifted the seat of her pajamas to a more acceptable spot and then locked the door to the bathroom. It had only been a few months since her older brother walked in on her and she wasn't about to take any chances of that happening again.

Erica stripped down as quickly as she could and shivered a bit in the growing cold. Her dad always fussed about the cost of heating their house and even though she could feel the warmth of air from the vents, the overall temperature was still too cold for being naked if she could avoid it. She started the water and tested it twice to get it to the right temperature before she caught her reflection in the mirror.

Her body was still short and bordered on pudgy as far as she was concerned. Erica accepted that she was never, ever going to be tall. Her skin was pale with a scattering of faint freckles that had happily faded since the summer. Her breasts were growing—she checked them every day in the hopes of some sort of miraculous explosion, but so far no luck—and that was as far as she got in her self-assessment.

The teeth marks on her breasts and sides threw her off checking the rest of her body. Erica stared for several seconds, her blue eyes growing wider in her face as she examined the marks. They stung a little, but they didn't really hurt. Most of the marks were red and fading, but a few of them were going to leave nasty bruises.

Erica gathered her clothes and ran from the bathroom, trying hard to bite back a scream. When she reached her bedroom she slammed the door and locked it. Normally her parents didn't like locked doors but right then she didn't care.

In her room she grabbed the mirror from her dressing stand and held it down close to her left breast, where she could see the reflection of the bite marks clearly. Whoever had bitten her had a small mouth, smaller than hers. The marks showed an even, straight set of teeth, except for the gap between the incisors. Not much of a gap, but it was there. She remembered it well. She'd seen that gap every time Tim smiled at her, and he'd smiled a lot.

Erica spent a good five minutes crying and screaming into her pillow, trying to recover from the fact that a nightmare had touched her, violated her. When she was a little calmer, she picked up the phone and started punching numbers. She was barely aware of what the numbers were, but she knew they were the right ones.

The phone rang three times before it was answered. "Hello?"

"Mr. Crowley?"

"That's the name. What can I do for you?"

"I don't know if you remember me, Mr. Crowley. My name is Erica Merriweather."

"Of course I remember you, Erica." His voice was pleasant, friendly. "What can I do for you?"

"Well, I think I've got a ghost that wants me to talk to you." That was as far as she got before the tears started.

Crowley listened to the girl and nodded his head. She'd been the one that got away back then when Tim got himself killed.

"No, Erica, you did exactly the right thing. Of course I'll try to help." He kept his voice soothing, because even over the phone line he could tell the girl was ready to break. Four years since Tim had died and according to her, he'd been haunting her dreams ever since. He and little dead Tim were going to have words, just as soon as he'd assessed the situation.

"Now, you said he bit you. Can you tell me where?" He grimaced as he shifted lanes. The address for Tim's mother wasn't very far away. "No, that doesn't sound like the Tim I met. But you have to understand, Erica, if he's really a ghost, he's probably very angry by now. Why? Because no one will listen to him. Well, you're listening now, yes, but this time he sent a very clear message, didn't he?"

He nodded patiently as the girl cried into the phone. As patiently as he could, at any rate. The entire situation was becoming annoying. He wanted to take care of his own business and now this was expanding into a first-class mess.

"Erica, honey, I'm about to pull up outside of your house. Yes, I told you I was close by. I wasn't exaggerating. Why don't you get dressed and come answer the door, okay?"

He disconnected the call and slid the phone into his pocket. The house was just waking up, which wasn't too surprising. It was only a little after seven in the morning and the sky was trying to convince the world that it was still midnight. The snow was still falling, sticking to the ground and everything around it.

Crowley climbed out of the driver's seat and stepped toward the house, taking his time and drinking in the chill in the air. There was no sign that a ghost was lingering around the neighborhood, but then, there seldom was. Most ghosts could hide away with ease. That was the part that pissed them off. They tended to hide too well and getting found became a challenge. Still, he looked around with altered perceptions and let himself see the dead.

There were no ghosts in the house in front of him. Two houses down on the right had a withered old man sitting on the porch and looking in his direction with moderate interest. As the man was dead, he didn't bother waving.

Another house down the way had a regular convention going on; seven men in biker's clothes, all of them dead, were gathered on the front lawn and talking. They were laughing, he could tell even from where he was. He sensed no malignance from them. Whatever they were doing, they weren't causing anyone any harm, at least not at the present.

That was it. The place was hardly a nexus for ghosts. He shivered a bit at the thought. He'd been around to see a few of the places that ghosts truly haunted. They were never a pleasant experience.

It was time to check on the girl. He moved through the thickening blanket of snow and knocked on the door, three sharp, hard raps.

A moment later a mid-forties man with a softening belly and a dazed expression on his face opened the door.

"Mr. Merriweather? Hi, I'm here to see Erica."

The man scowled. It wasn't anger on his face; it was confusion. "Erica?"

"You know, your daughter?"

The man nodded and stepped back from the door. "Come on in, I'll get her." For the first time, there was a hint of suspicion in the man's voice. That suited Crowley just fine. More parents should be concerned about their kids and their safety. Maybe then there wouldn't be so much work for him.

When the man came back down a few moments later, a woman trailed him, close to his own age, who stared at Crowley for a moment before she recognized him. The girl, who looked much more like her mother than she had when she was younger, stayed between the two parents.

"How are you, Sarah?" Crowley smiled thinly. The woman blanched a bit. They'd left on unusual terms and she'd likely never expected to see him again.

"Jonathan?" She moved two steps in his direction and then stopped herself.

"It's nice to see you again, Sarah. Has everything been all right here?"

Mr. Merriweather was starting to look confused and annoyed, which seemed fair as the last time Crowley had been around the man had been in Europe on business.

"This must be your husband, Ned, right?" Crowley smiled and offered his hand. Merriweather thought it over for a second and shook.

"Ned, Jonathan Crowley is the man that helped us when the Daniels's had their problems a few years ago."

The man yanked his hand away as if he'd been scalded.

Crowley didn't take offense. He knew better.

"Oh. You're that guy."

Jonathan smiled. Ned backed off unconsciously. Crowley's smile had that effect on a lot of people.

"Your daughter here gave me a call. Seems she's having some troubles with the Daniels' family again."

"I don't want to hear about this." Ned shook his head and walked away, the scowl of confusion never leaving his face. Denial in the face of unusual circumstances. Crowley dealt with it regularly. Frankly, it made his life a little easier. Hysteria was a pain in the ass, but denial was just sort of comforting: it proved him right in his assessments of the average person. Stupidity and denial were about what he expected.

Sarah Merriweather looked at him expectantly. "What do you need with Erica?"

"Not a blessed thing. She called me."

"Why did she call you?"

Crowley shrugged. "Tell you what. Why don't I give you two a few minutes to play mom and daughter? I'll just stand here in the doorway and let the snow creep on into your house, I mean, it's your heating bill, not mine."

Sarah flushed a bit. "I'm sorry, Mr. Crowley. Why don't you come inside? I can get you a cup of coffee if you'd like."

He nodded, stepped through the doorway and closed the door. "That'd be great."

No sooner had the woman grabbed her daughter's arm and headed for the kitchen than his phone rang again.

"Better be important," he answered.

"Jonathan? It's Amelia."

"How are things, Amelia? What can I do for you?"

"I found a few more books."

"Yeah, I figured Vernon had a couple socked away somewhere. I was planning on coming by when I was done with the things I have to handle."

"That's good. It would be nice to see you."

"What's the point of the call, Amelia?" The books were an excuse and he knew it. Despite everything she'd seen over the years, Amelia still didn't think the books could really be dangerous. She was naïve like that.

"Jonathan, I found my father's address books, too. I think he might have known something about—"

He waited for her to keep talking. He waited a little longer while he heard the sounds of mother and daughter arguing in the next room.

When he grew tired of waiting, he asked again, his impatience obvious in his voice. "About what, Amelia? I don't have all day."

"About who killed your family."

Jonathan Crowley closed his eyes and kept them that way for several seconds. His teeth clenched savagely and his pulse hammered in his skull.

"What did you say, Amelia?"

"I think he knew who killed Elizabeth and the children, Jonathan. I'm so sorry."

"Give me a name."

"What?"

"Give me a name, Amelia. It might confirm something for me."

"Robert Workham." Her voice trembled as she spoke.

"Thank you. We'll talk soon."

"Jonathan!" He cut off her voice and folded the phone back into his pocket.

When he opened his eyes again, he seemed perfectly calm. Amelia Dunlow would have known better.

Sarah Merriweather came toward him with a cup of coffee in a plastic travel mug.

He smiled as he took it from her. A small smile, the sort that didn't make the woman want to flinch too much. No point in seeing her get all covered in the drink he was looking forward to.

"Thank you, Sarah. Now, you have two choices, same as before. I help you, or I don't. Your decision."

She looked back at the kitchen where Erica was sitting at the table, crying softly.

"Yes, Mr. Crowley. I'd like your help."

Crowley smiled again and nodded. "Excellent. Why don't we go in the kitchen and have ourselves a little chat, okay?"

Bob poured himself another cup of coffee and looked at his family. Once again the swell of pride filled him. How had he ever managed to get so lucky?

He looked away from them as he scowled. He wasn't really sure if luck had anything to do with it. More like determination.

And it was determination that made him decide to try calling Albert Miles himself. He needed to make his final payment, to get everything taken care of if he wanted to have a normal, human, life.

If it was even possible. He thought it was. He hoped it was. And yet, just a few hours ago, when his family was sleeping, he'd gone out in the night again, hunted, killed and devoured not only the flesh but the soul of another human being.

He forced a smile as the guilt washed over him. Love. Guilt. Human emotions, surely. No demon had ever suffered from either to the best of his knowledge.

Amy came over and crawled in her father's lap. "Hi, Daddy!"

The guilt vanished in an instant, replaced by the warmth that washed through him whenever his children were around.

"Hey, baby girl." Amy was five, just a baby, and an innocent. The girl he'd killed last night? She had been older, probably already hooked on heroin or something worse. Really, he'd done the girl a favor. He'd stopped her from enduring years of misery at the hands of her pimp, and he'd left the man who sold her to strangers bloodied and ruined.

He tried hard to justify himself, but then he thought of Amy. Five now, yes, but how long until she became the object of someone's desire? The thought sickened most of him, but there was that infernal aspect that nearly cackled with joy at the notion of Amy suffering so dearly.

Bob pulled her from his lap and into his arms, hugging her fiercely but carefully. Drinking in the scent of her baby shampoo and the warmth of her innocence. The idea of anyone ever hurting her sent shivers through his mind and, dare he say it, his soul.

He'd kill anyone who ever hurt Amy, or Bobby, or Steve. He'd destroy them as surely as he'd killed before.

And there it was, the guilt, coming back with a vengeance. He'd killed before, murdered people who had done nothing to him, too many to count, really, after centuries of servitude to sorcerers who demanded services and paid with the lives of other people. A precious commodity, as Bob was learning.

Colleen came over and placed her hand on his shoulder. She'd grown used to his ways, odd though they sometimes seemed to her, and she loved him. He could feel that with every gesture she made.

They'd had long talks about their pasts, and in those talks he'd lied through his teeth, explaining that he had done a few things he was ashamed of when he was younger, but never, not even for a moment, considering telling her the truth of the matter.

"Breakfast is ready." Colleen leaned down and rested her chin on the top of his head. Strange, how a simple and rather silly gesture always brought him comfort. Just the touch of her against him, and the tensions eased.

In the other room, Bobby and Steve were watching cartoons. It was a snow day and they intended to make the most of it. That would change in a minute. The first rule of the Workham household was that meals were taken together, in the kitchen or in the dining room. There were no exceptions made for snow days.

He'd already called the office and said he couldn't make it in. Then he'd called back and told everyone to have a day off. With pay. Now and then he could afford to be extravagant, and a happy office was a productive office.

He turned his head up and kissed Colleen's lips. She smiled into the kiss and her eyes promised they'd find some time alone later, when the children were properly looked after.

And there it was again, that feeling of love. My, how good it felt: how wonderfully, amazingly human and natural.

He wanted it to last forever. He'd make it last forever.

A phone call after breakfast then, to find out where Albert Miles was hiding himself. Anything at all. He'd do anything at all to keep the family and the life that he'd carved for himself in a world he wasn't even supposed to be a part of.

He'd kill a thousand people if that's what it took. A thousand lives. Not really that many in the grander scheme of things.

Bob lifted his little girl and settled her on his waist as he headed for the kitchen and breakfast.

Pancakes and sausage, scrambled eggs, another cup of coffee. A little slice of paradise, really. So many went hungry these days. So many suffered. He would take all of the joys he could for his family and do everything he could to make sure they never joined the sufferers.

Amelia's flight landed in Chicago despite the bad weather. She had a few moments when she was afraid things would go wrong, but in the long run, all was well.

She didn't bother with a cab. She got a limo instead. She'd done her share of roughing it over the years, and frankly, she wanted a little comfort.

Mike was upset with her, but not too upset. He didn't understand her attachment to Jonathan, but he forgave it. That was really the only way she could define the situation. He understood, though it took a while, that there was nothing unusual between the two of them. More importantly, though it often seemed that way to people who didn't know them, there was nothing sexual.

The chauffeur did his best to keep his eyes on the road and not on her. Just to make sure he got the point, she closed the darkened window between them, the better to keep him from getting distracted.

She knew where she was going, knew she had to get there, but didn't like the idea very much. Jonathan would be hunting down Robert Workham just as surely as he'd hunt down anything that hurt a loved one.

She remembered the murders well enough. She'd been much younger then, though few would be able to see the difference in her features. Still, she remembered when Jonathan vanished from the face of the earth and the subsequent investigations into the deaths of his entire family.

Her father had been the one to insist on investigating the situation himself. Despite their differences, he understood that he owed a great deal to Jonathan Crowley. Jonathan had let him live. Had let Amelia live, despite the demonic essences inside of her.

Sometimes she suspected he regretted that decision, which was why coming to see him now was a terrifying prospect. It was impossible to know him, to really understand him, and she'd been trying for a very long time.

She could read emotions, that was one of her gifts. She could always read whatever was coming from Jonathan, unless he shut himself off from her, but knowing what he was feeling on the surface wasn't like understanding the depths of his emotions and even when she got a clear picture of how he was feeling, his actions seldom matched up with what she read from him.

She shivered, despite the warmth of the limousine. Jonathan Crowley was a scary man. That was all there was to it. She knew there was more to him, but his life was violent, tumultuous, and filled with horrors she didn't like to think about too much.

He did, though. He thought about them all the time. It was his escape, she knew, from the pain he still felt when he thought back over the decades. By now his children would have had children of their own and he would have been long dead if things hadn't worked out the way they had. He had not aged gracefully when he had aged, and that didn't seem to bother him in the least. He'd reveled in being old, in being decrepit and crippled, as some people would love to find the fountain of youth.

Jonathan didn't need the fountain. Ponce de Leon might have been on a quest for it, but Jonathan already had the gift of eternal life or something close enough that he didn't seem to mind much.

No, that was a lie. He hated it. At least some of the time.

The rest of the time he was hunting monsters and heaping abuse on the people around him.

She shook her head and pushed that notion out of her head. Most of them deserved the abuse. That was the sort of people he ran across regularly. People like, well, like her father. People who delved into dangerous areas and ran the risk of causing more damage than good with their explorations.

To her knowledge, Vernon Dunlow had never hurt anyone, but he had consorted with demons and judging by some of the comments in his address books, he'd know a great number of very dangerous individuals. He had made a fortune for himself by dealing with the wrong people, the wrong entities in the eyes of Jonathan Crowley and, unlike most of the people who had followed that path, he'd lived to tell the tale.

But this? Knowing that he had known about exactly who had committed the atrocities against his family? How would Jonathan handle the news?

She didn't know and she was afraid to know. Still, Jonathan had been there for her through almost every trial in her life, and now she had to see him, to make him understand before he did anything rash. What if the man wasn't the right person? What if he was completely innocent?

And why hadn't he sounded at all surprised when she told him the news?

"Jonathan, what are you doing in Chicago?"

She asked the question aloud just to hear someone talk.

She dreaded the answer.

Jonathan Crowley had rules he followed, the same as everyone else, everything else, really. There were certain stipulations to his power, because nothing comes without a price.

Stepping outside of those boundaries could get him badly hurt and possibly even killed. Amelia wasn't quite ready to face the world without him in it, and so she was in Chicago, heading toward the house of a potentially very dangerous individual.

She had to try to save Jonathan, even if she got herself killed in the process.

Annoyed didn't even start to cover it. Pissed off, infuriated, inconvenienced in a bad way, sure. But annoyed wasn't a tenth of what he was feeling.

In a perfect world, he'd be enjoying himself right now, taking out four decades of fury on a certain demon. Instead, he was delaying his satisfaction because of his duties.

Jonathan Crowley was in a bad mood.

He looked at the house on Wickhaven Street and sighed through his nose. The Daniels' house had been lovely once, but these days it was looking decrepit. The lawn was a wild jungle of crab grass and weeds that actually stuck out of the growing snow; and under the layer of frozen precipitation that was trying to bury it, Crowley could see the peeling paint of the house and on the porch as well.

That wasn't the part that bothered him, however. It was the strong aura of desperation and pain that surrounded the premises that left him infuriated.

That sort of emotional stew almost guaranteed that someone had been getting stupid. He didn't like stupid people. They made his life difficult, to say the least.

The girl, Erica, was in the seat next to him. Her mother was in the back of the car. Why? Because the girl annoyed him less and he actually needed her there to fix the problem. Mom was just being a protective mother, and therefore a pain in his ass.

Four years had passed since someone in the neighborhood had played with things best left alone and ripped a pinhole rift between worlds. It wouldn't have been a problem if that same someone hadn't managed to seal the rift so that it stayed open.

Crowley had come in to set things right, because that was what he was supposed to do. Unfortunately, he wasn't fast enough to stop a few people from getting killed in the process, and that included Tim Daniels. He'd managed to screw up saving the kid by something like ten seconds and that was something he just had to deal with. He wasn't the one that opened a hole in the universe; he was just the one that got stuck patching it. As long as he reminded himself of that little fact from time to time, he didn't feel too much like pounding his fists into walls.

Erica chewed at her nails. Crowley slapped her hand lightly. "Knock it off. No one likes messy nails."

She looked at him for a second, and then nodded.

"So, let's get this done, okay? You're here for a reason, and I'm here to see that you stay safe. That means you don't get to do anything except stand there." He spoke to Erica. Sarah opened her mouth and he turned to her quickly before word one escaped her lips. "We had an arrangement, didn't we? You get to stand with Erica and say nothing, do nothing. That's the arrangement. Want to break the rules, and we can make a new arrangement."

Sarah shut her mouth. That was for the best. The unfinished business between them was in the past and he intended to keep it that way.

Crowley climbed out of his car and the two women followed him. He looked over the house carefully as he approached and shook his head. Laura Daniels had been a nice woman, friendly and gentle with her son. Now, four years later, he was dreading seeing what time had done to her.

He could understand her pain all too well, of course. He'd lost three children and a wife in one day. That thought simply brought back the reasons he had for being damned annoyed by the calls he'd received.

Don't think of it as being delayed. Think of it as time to plan far more devastating tortures. He used the words as a personal mantra to keep him going.

He didn't bother with preamble, but simply knocked sharply on the door.

No one answered the first time so he hit the door harder until he finally got a response.

The woman that answered the door barely even resembled the Laura Daniels he had met in the past. Her skin was pale and splotchy. Her dark, beautiful eyes were looking a bit jaundiced. The figure she'd worked so hard to keep was gone, replaced by an emaciated scarecrow's form in a dress that was at least three sizes too large, and the glorious hair he'd admired when he met her had mutated into a mess of tangles and knots that would likely never be combed out without a few locks being cut away.

He knew the signs well enough. Whether by demon or ghost, Laura Daniels was being hag-ridden. An older term, true enough, but one that still fit. Depression is a bad enough thing and could have caused all of the symptoms he was looking at. He might well have looked at her and decided that she was suffering from something that was beyond his ability to help, but the smile on her face, the one that showed her diseased gums and the teeth that were threatening to fall from her mouth, convinced him otherwise.

Somewhere within her home, a demon or a spirit of some kind was using the woman in front of him to feed on, draining her life force away and judging by the dreamy grin on her ruined face, the same being was giving her false happiness in exchange. Not a symbiotic relationship, but a parasitic one. Left to her own devices, she'd be dead within a month and to add insult to injury, she was probably convinced that the entity was her son, returned from the dead.

For just a moment, a deep sorrow washed through him. He felt for her, empathized with the desires to have Tim back in her life. His death had hit her harder than he realized, than he wanted to think about.

Then he brushed the pity aside and let the anger fill him. It was very, very rare for a spirit to enter a house and attach itself to a single person without an invitation of some sort. Not impossible, but rare, especially in cases where the damage was so noticeable. In most cases, the ghosts that linked themselves to a person weren't strong enough to do any lasting damage. That meant what he was dealing with was probably a demon.

"Oh, Laura." He shook his head and sighed. "Why the hell did you have to go and get stupid?"

Laura Daniels turned her face toward him, her eyes still sparkling with false joy. "I know you, don't I?" She nodded to herself and he could see the veil drop over her eyes. "Yes, you're the one who saved Tim!"

She took a step toward him, her thin arms reaching out as if to give him a hug. Crowley stepped back and shook his head. He didn't want to get thanks from her for failing, whether she believed he'd saved her son or not.

"No, Laura. I didn't." His voice was softer than usual, but only a little.

The woman stepped back, a crafty expression sliding across her features. "He's not here right now."

"Who's not here?"

"Tim."

"Are you sure? Because Erica came to see him."

Laura's sunken eyes rolled for a moment and the crafty expression faded away, replaced by a ghost of her previous beauty as she relaxed into a smile. "Erica! Oh, he'll be so happy that you're here! I know he's been wanting to see you!"

She slid past him, the stench of her unwashed body assailing him as she reached for the girl. Erica flinched, understandably, but did as Jonathan had requested and stood her ground, forcing a smile as fake as any seasoned politician's.

"Hi, Missus Daniels. Can Tim come out to play?"

"Well of *course* he can! He'll be so thrilled to see you!" She turned around with a surprising amount of animation and called out, "Tim! Wait 'til you see who came here to see you!"

Crowley felt it coming, but saw nothing. The air in the room changed, grew heavier and colder as something approached them. At the threshold of the door, Erica started to step back, and he held up a single finger to remind her that she was still needed, at least for a little longer. Her mother let out a soft moan of fear that he ignored completely. She had every reason to be afraid. Her daughter's life was at stake.

Jonathan Crowley then stood perfectly still, save to whisper a few words under his breath. The spell was simple and effective and hid him from view until he moved again. He saw the look of surprise on Erica's face from the corner of his eye, but couldn't do anything to let her know all was well, not just yet.

Tim Daniels manifested in the room. He stepped forward from thin air, looking as healthy and happy as he had four years earlier, before he'd been torn apart. He heard the gasps from mother and daughter alike, and saw the way Laura's tragic smile grew broader, happier.

And then he looked at Tim again and saw him for what he was. An imp: a minor demon at best. The beast looked like little more than a cloud of filth, surrounded by floating streamers of pale energies that ran directly into the body of Laura Daniels. He could see the links that bound the creature to Laura, the brilliant flashes of light that no one could see under normal circumstances, which ran from the woman to the creature in a continuous feed. It wasn't just feeding on her; it was devouring her at a savage rate. She could have summoned it as little as a month before with the way it was consuming her soul.

"Tim?" Erica's voice was shocked. It was one thing to be haunted by a memory and another to see a boy she knew was dead walking toward her, as real and lively as he had ever been.

Crowley watched for a moment as the trails of energy that hovered around Laura slithered toward the teenager. It never lost its grip on Tim Daniels' mother, but it most certainly intended to feed off of Erica, the greedy little shit.

He wasn't about to let that happen.

Crowley reached out for the closest shimmering line of energies and clutched it in his hand. The spell that had hidden him away dissolved as it was meant to, and the demon recoiled as his hand locked down on the conduit it wanted to use for raping the soul of a little girl.

Anger flared through Crowley as he smiled and ripped the tendril away from the imp. The energy stream shattered, dissolving as it fell away and Tim Daniels let out a shriek of agony that caused the two visiting women to flinch and Laura to let out a wail of her own as she reached for her son.

Before she could touch the vile thing again, Crowley intervened, moving his hands and speaking under his breath, summoning the power to destroy the attachment between mother and imposter son.

Laura's eyes flew wide and she screamed again, a raw, desperate cry of pain, and fell to her knees, her body trembling.

The imp screamed too, not in pain or loss, but in rage. Tim's sweet, ten-year-old face twisted and warped, revealing his true nature to the people around him and Tim, a gentle soul in life, leaped for Crowley's throat while baring teeth that had hidden in a mouth too large for his face.

The transformation didn't stop there. Even in mid-leap it was possible to see the soft, pale flesh change, growing darker as Tim was replaced by the imp's physical form.

Might have worked with most people. Jonathan Crowley caught the thing by its throat and pinned it to the wall with ease. He smiled as the creature clawed at his arms and tore flesh and clothing. Oh, to be sure it hurt and he wanted to scream in pain, but that was a part of the job and there was very little that could cause Crowley permanent harm.

"You're hurting me, you little shit." His voice was a purr and his smile grew broader still.

The creature clawed and tried to bite and he let it for another few seconds as he assessed the situation.

And then he destroyed the beast. It had taken physical form, manifested itself into the world, and he let it, knowing that it was the most vulnerable when it could cause physical damage.

Crowley held the imp by its neck and used his other hand to clutch its skull in his fingers. The demon's eyes flew wide as he applied more force until the fingers in its throat were nearly pressed together and the skull of the thing started to crack.

From her position on the ground, Laura let out another scream, an incoherent battle cry as she crawled toward the demon that had fooled her and the man who was so obviously killing it.

Crowley scowled and squeezed harder until the bones under his fingertips broke open and the black filth within the imp was released. At the same time, he spoke the words of a simple binding spell that held the spirit within the form and then dropped the dead body to the ground.

Laura wasn't interested in examining her dead son. She had other ideas in mind, including trying her best to kill Jonathan Crowley.

She lunged for him, her teeth bared, her eyes wild, and tried to bite him in a place no man wants to have used as a chew toy.

There had been more than a few occasions in the past when he was in a charitable mood, or even caught off guard, and he let someone attack him.

He wasn't feeling very charitable, so instead he bent his leg at the knee and kicked the woman squarely in her face.

She crumbled to the ground for a second time and sobbed into her hands. Thin trails of blood slipped between her clutching fingers and

Crowley stared down at her, the rage inside of him boiling closer to the surface.

On the ground to his left, a broken woman softly cried out her sorrows. To his right, the body of a demon decomposed, melting into a thick tar-like substance. Within five minutes, he knew that the demon's form would be completely gone. He also knew that if he let the body be, the energies that made up the demon would be freed again.

Crowley reached down and sank his fingers into the withering corpse, catching the spirit and pulling it into his clenched hand. The thing burned, seared his skin and struggled desperately to get free, but he held it too tightly, refusing to let it go.

There would be no sympathy today, not for the demon, not for the woman, and not for the last player in the game he'd been called in to referee.

Not for the ghost of Tim Daniels, who had been tormenting a little girl for the last four years.

"Oh my God! You hit her!" Sarah's voice was shocked.

Crowley didn't even bother looking at the woman. "Yes, as a matter of fact, I did."

"But, why?"

Crowley looked her way and Sarah stepped back. "Where do you want me to start?"

"But she, her son…"

"Son's dead. Been haunting your daughter, remember?"

"But you didn't have to hit her."

"She was going to attack me." He spoke slowly, resisting the urge to thump the woman on the top of her head. "She was going to do things like bite me in the leg and maybe try to scratch my testicles out of existence. Have you ever been bitten in the leg?"

"Well, no."

"Then you don't know how much that shit hurts, do you?"

Erica stared at the two of them, her mouth hanging open. She had the shakes again, and her skin was both pale and sweaty.

Crowley stared at the girl and tried to focus on what, if anything, might be around her. He hadn't seen anything earlier, but now the circumstances were different. If Tim was going to show himself, it would be soon.

"You still shouldn't have hit her." Sarah crossed her arms and did her best to glare a hole through his head.

"Really, Sarah?" He stared back, his smile broadening. "You think I should have just left a demon eating her soul? Or would it be better just to walk away right now, while everything's been half done?"

"What?" Panic lifted her voice a couple of octaves. "You wouldn't!"

"Watch me, sweet pea. I've got other things to attend to right now."

"You'd leave her like this?" The shock echoed through each word she spoke and her face took on the start of an angry expression.

Crowley took two steps and leaned down to look her in her eyes from a few inches apart. "In a heartbeat. Just a ghost, really. She'd probably teach herself to ignore it, given enough time."

"You're a bastard!"

"Yes, I am. Comes with the territory. Now either shut up and let me do my job or I'll gladly call it all done. How's that sound to you, precious?"

"STOP IT!" Crowley and both women turned to where Erica stood, her body shivering in the cold from the open door. "Stop it, Mom! He's helping us!"

"He never helps anyone, Erica!" Sarah jabbed a finger in Crowley's direction, her pretty face marred by the anger that added lines to her face and aged her by a decade or more. In that moment she looked almost as bitter as Crowley felt. "He claims to help them, but look at what happened to Tim! Look at what happened to poor Laura! If he'd helped them back then, none of this would be happening."

And there it was, the bitter truth of the matter. He failed as often as he succeeded. That fact alone had been the cause of plenty of sleepless nights. He hadn't saved everyone in Serenity Falls, or in London, or in any of Europe when he'd walked there. He'd dropped the ball in Sri Lanka and Rome and Red Rock. The list went on and on.

Crowley looked down at Sarah and shook his head. "You're on your own. Go find yourself someone who can make it all better."

Without another word, he walked across the threshold of the house and into the snow, past the woman and then past her daughter. Erica reached for him, her hands clawing at his jacket, desperate to get him to stop.

"You said you'd help me, Mr. Crowley! You said you'd make him stop." Her voice broke and even without looking at her, he could imagine the tears starting in her eyes.

"Yeah?" He made sure not to turn around. If he looked at the girl, he'd waver. "Your mother doesn't want my help. Anything I do to you might be frowned on in a court of law, so I'm leaving."

Erica's hands let go of his jacket and he heard the sound of her sharp intake. The breath was released in a shuddering moan and he started walking. Not daring to look at her.

Sarah ran past her daughter and reached for him, surely just as intent as Laura had been on punishing him for his actions.

And in the hallway of the house he'd just left, Laura Daniels spoke softly, her voice giving a small glimmer of hope in all the wretchedness. "Tim? Honey? Is it really you?"

Crowley grabbed Sarah's hands and pinned them with his own. She flinched and then struggled, desperate to get away from him, but he refused to let her go. The essence of the demonic imp burned in the palm of his hand and seared both him and the woman who'd taken all of her feelings for him and let them sour in her heart.

"Let me go! I hate you, Jonathan! I hate you!"

Crowley grinned a feral, wild snarl of a smile and whispered too softly for Erica to hear, "Did you tell good old Ned about what you tried to do with me in your marriage bed, Sarah? Did you let him know about that? Is that why he left the room when I got there, kitten?"

Sarah's face reddened and shame changed her features, made her lovely where anger had marred her. "You go to Hell, Jonathan!"

He let go of one of her arms and as she tried to pull away, he reeled her back in, spinning her until she faced away from him and looked into the semidarkness of the Daniels home foyer.

Her body struggled against him, her backside to his front, her arms scratching at his jacket even as he held her chin and made her look at the wretch on the ground, looking up into the shadows to see what death had done to her son.

Tim Daniels looked at his mother, half prone on the ground and thus the same height as him. The dead boy was evident at last. He'd waited, of course, until the Hunter was gone and promising not to return. He wasn't a foolish boy, only dead. He understood that once Crowley had been asked, he could do as he pleased. What he didn't understand was that once an invitation was given, it couldn't be revoked. Jonathan Crowley had said he would leave, but he had not done so. He'd merely played the part well enough to fool a dead boy.

Sarah flinched again, this time leaning into Crowley, shaking her head as if she could, through force of will, deny the reality of what she was seeing.

She'd attended the funeral of little Tim Daniels, had done her best to comfort Laura and then done her best to forget the incident entirely.

And in the process, she'd ignored the dreams of her only daughter, brushed them aside as delusions.

Crowley's voice was a burning hiss in her ear. "See him, Sarah? See what happened to Tim? You knew about it, didn't you? You knew he wasn't resting, because Erica told you about him and what did you do, dear, sweet Sarah? You sent her to a shrink and paid her bills and pretended nothing bad ever happened around here."

"Jonathan, please, I didn't know." Her voice broke as she talked, her eyes watered.

Crowley's body pressed against hers and she let out a moan. There was nothing sexual in his motions, merely a shift of his body as he prepared to do what he had to do.

"Lie all you want, if it makes you feel better, sweetheart, but I know the truth. I can see it written on your face." Oh, how his voice dripped with venom and hatred. "Maybe you didn't really see Tim, but you knew about him. You could have called me and I'd have come running four years ago, but instead you had to worry about what Ned would say if he met me. You had to think about yourself and screw everything else."

Sarah shook her head and tried to find the words to deny what he said.

"How many nights did Erica wake up screaming because you didn't want to deal with me again, Sarah? How many fucking doctors did you make her go see?"

Erica let out a sob and backed away from the door as Tim stepped more directly into the light. A lot of times, light made the ghosts of the world fade away, but not now, not this time. Tim had gained power now, not only over his childhood friend, but finally, at long last, over his mother as well. True, the demon had lied to her—all demons lie, really, it's in their nature—but it had touched her perceptions enough to allow her to see her son's spirit at last.

"Four years, Sarah. Four years while Tim tried to make his mother see him and used Erica as a means to an end. He might have loved your daughter once, but death makes a ghost greedy for contact, greedy for life. He fed on Erica because she could see him, and when he wasn't using your daughter to keep him strong, he came here and begged his mother to see him again, to love him again."

"No...No, it wasn't like that. It couldn't be like that." Sarah shook her head again and again as the tears fell in earnest.

"Just last night he bit your daughter's breasts hard enough to leave bruises, Sarah. Hard enough to leave physical marks. Do you know how difficult that is for a ghost to accomplish?"

Tim Daniels touched his mother's hair and his fingers moved the matted strands. Most ghosts would never have the power to affect the living, but the ones that did, Crowley knew from long experience, were some of the most dangerous creatures in existence. Isolation and despair made them bitter. Bitterness festered and became hatred and hatred, oh, hatred was the fuel that let them do the most unspeakable things...

"Four years, Sarah, and you knew where to reach me, knew I'd have come back and stopped it. Four years of letting Laura wallow in her misery and grow sick enough to call a demon to raise her son from the dead. Four years of poor, sweet Erica being defiled by her dead friend. Yesterday he touched your daughter's body, sweet pea, but he's been *raping* her *soul* for four miserable years."

Crowley shoved her then and Sarah fell forward, crying out at last as she fell into the snow.

Laura Daniels turned at the sudden outcry, so did Erica and so, too, did Tim Daniels. Tim had thought the Hunter gone, because he'd left the house. All he wanted was what he now had, the mother he'd been seeking since his violent death.

The sweet face of a ten-year-old innocent looked out from the foyer, but the mask was thin now, and the corruption was easily seen. The wounds of death showed on Tim's face and body, the decay of his spirit manifested as blackened shadows that distorted his face and devoured his flesh.

Tim Daniels looked at Jonathan Crowley and roared. The windows of the house where he'd lived buckled and shattered at the sound, and the snow that rested on the roof slid down in a blinding cascade that half hid ruined mother and dead child alike.

Erica screamed and tried to run away, but the snow was too deep and her panic too bright. She slipped and fell and crawled through the snow, moving as she always did to the woman who'd raised her and always comforted her; the woman who had, in time, failed to protect her.

Jonathan Crowley stepped past mother and daughter and headed back for the house, his smile a slash of white against his pale face.

"Hey, Tim. Look at this. You managed to get someone to help you after all."

"Go away!" The voice was too deep, too loud to come from a little boy.

"Can't do that, Tim. See, Erica asked *me* to help *her* get rid of *you*. You've been a very naughty boy."

"I won't see her anymore, I promise." Clever ghost, it tried to hide away the anger and show only the innocent it had been once upon a time. The face that peered out of the house with the broken windows was all innocence and light, a face that still haunted Jonathan Crowley on nights when he was alone and contemplating the past.

"No, Tim. It's too late for that." The thrill was gone and when Crowley spoke it was softly, with regret.

"I won't hurt anyone else, I promise!" Oh, how the ghost begged. His eyes were wide, his face sincere and the worst of it was, Crowley knew that Tim meant every word. Still, he couldn't take that chance. Tim Daniels had grown strong already in death, and given time he could grow far too powerful.

"I'm sorry, Tim. I mean that." He spoke the words softly, because it wouldn't do to let anyone around him know he had feelings. Crowley lunged forward and grabbed the boy, his fingers feelings resistance as ectoplasm fought to gain true cohesion in the world of the living. Tim tried to struggle, tried to fight, but really, Crowley had already bested a demon a thousand times more powerful.

A moment later Tim's scream faded away and what was left of his soul was held clutched in Crowley's hand, bound within the wards he summoned to hold the spirit of a troubled dead boy.

"No mercy today, Tim. I can't afford it right now. Nothing personal."

He could only hold the spirits for so long. They caused him pain, and with or without the ability to heal, he had limits as to how much he wanted to endure. Still, a few moments longer he could manage without trouble, the better to deal with Laura Daniels.

Finding her was easy enough. She hadn't moved much at all, save to curl in on herself. Laura had her eyes open, but there was no one at home inside of her. He'd seen the look enough times to understand it, and found himself wondering if she'd survive long enough to recover.

He stepped into the house, ignoring the women both inside and out. A few minutes was all it took for him to locate the summoning spell she'd used in an attempt to resurrect her son.

The summoning spell was written on notebook paper and he recognized the handwriting easily enough. The late Marvin Daniels, deceased husband of Laura, who'd started all of the nightmares her family had faced to begin with.

"I'll be taking this with me, Laura." He spoke softly and offered her no assistance.

"Go to hell." Her voice was broken, and weak, little more than a whisper.

"You'll get better, Laura. I know you don't believe me, but you will. It just takes time."

"You took my boy from me."

"No, Laura. I didn't. He's been gone for four years." He wanted to be angry with her, wanted to scream and rant, but he didn't have it in him. There were too many similarities for him. She'd suffered the loss of everyone who mattered to her and it had broken her. He just hoped she'd give herself a chance to get fixed.

The woman made no further comments, and after a moment he left her alone in her misery. There was too much to do and he was already very tired.

The snow was still falling and outside the two women he'd brought with him huddled together looking miserable and scared.

"You can come with me now, or you can walk home." He stared at Sarah as he spoke. "Personally, I don't much care which."

After a moment of looking at each other, mother and daughter rose from the snow and headed for his car.

He drove them back to their home in silence and left as soon as they climbed free.

Amelia stood in the cold and waited outside of the Workham house. It hadn't been difficult to find, especially since the driver knew his way around.

The limo was behind her, idling. The driver was talking on his cell phone and she could feel his desire as he looked at her. So far at least, he was keeping himself in check. He had a vile mind and a sick imagination, but he was behaving.

She hoped he kept it that way.

It would likely not be long before Jonathan showed up. She couldn't pinpoint his location through the population around her, but she could still sense him and his rage.

He was so very, very angry.

His fury kept her warm as the snow continued to fall.

Jonathan Crowley pulled up a half block away from the Workham place. He stared at the house through the curtain of falling snow and listened to his heartbeat thunder in his chest.

He'd seen Amelia, of course, but he didn't feel the need to talk to her. She'd just say something stupid to him about not hurting anyone.

The thought brought a thin smile to his face.

He stared at the two entities he'd bound to himself. The demon still struggled. The ghost of a boy he'd failed did not fight, but only, he was sure, because Tim Daniels was terrified.

The rules had changed when Tim wasn't looking and in the long run, ghost or not, he was still only a boy.

"Time to go, Tim. Time to move on." He cast the spirit away and into the "light" that so many claimed to see. He didn't bother to see if he could find what was beyond that light or where Tim would eventually end up. In the first place, he wasn't that interested in knowing, and in the second, he'd never once managed to find out where the dead went when they finally escaped their own pain and suffering.

He still tried now and then, but not as often as he used to. Why torment himself with possibilities that were beyond his reach? He had enough reasons to be angry already.

He was not as gentle with the imp. He used that spirit to test a theory of his instead. To date, at least two demons that he had defeated had managed to come back for more and he wasn't very fond of that notion. So he tried something new and bound the imp with spells he had seldom used before. When he was done, the creature was still screaming, still suffering in agony. The sounds made him smile. Later, possibly, he'd see about banishing it properly, but for now the sounds made him happy.

A moment later, he climbed from his car and started down the block. If Amelia saw him she never gave any indication of it.

The house was a nice one; split level with room to spare and nice, sensible earth tones. It didn't look like it belonged to a demon, or like it should be granted to a murderer.

Crowley circled the place slowly, careful to stay out of view of both the inhabitants and the woman who was, doubtless, there to protect him from himself.

He saw the family in the living room, sitting on a large, comfy couch. There was a striking woman dressed in jeans and a simple blouse and three children surrounding her. He watched them for several moments, feeling the familiar ache of loss blow through his soul.

A lifetime had passed for a lot of people and he still missed them, the sounds of their laughter, the scent of his children coming in from the summer heat, the feel of Elizabeth's hand touching his face when she smiled up at him. Every day he missed them.

He stared for several moments, until he could sense the woman growing uncomfortable. That happened sometimes. There were those people who almost always knew when they were being watched, even if they couldn't see anyone.

He spotted the man of the house pacing in the hallway, peering in from time to time with a preoccupied look on his face.

He looked nothing like the man who had murdered Crowley's family, but it wasn't impossible to hide the truth from him, just difficult.

He stared long and hard and memorized every detail of the man's face. Then, when he had all of the visual confirmation he could hope for, Jonathan Crowley paid a visit.

Breakfast was done and the family was watching a movie, *The Little Mermaid* on DVD, which remained one of Amy's favorites though she had surely seen it a hundred times or more. Neither of the boys complained, because afterwards, if the weather was still as miserable, he'd promised them they could watch *Pirates of the Caribbean*.

Bob was on the phone, trying for the tenth time to get through to Albert Miles. So far it was nothing but voicemails and he was starting to get worried. He wanted this done, one way or another.

The knock at the door was unexpected and unwanted. Bob scowled a bit and looked toward the living room where his family watched the big screen TV and munched on popcorn.

Colleen looked his way and asked him silently to answer the door and he nodded and forced a smile as he went to see who was knocking in the middle of a blizzard. Likely it was Curt Fulford from next door. Curt was a nice guy, but almost always wanted to borrow something. Normally the man would be working in his garage on whatever he decided to build next. Bob envied Curt his craftsmen skills and Curt envied him his collection of power tools. It worked out well enough between the two of them. Thanks to the numerous loans over the years, Curt had been the one to help him refinish the back porch over the course of the summer.

Bob opened the door at exactly the same time Albert Miles spoke into his ear. Well, the recorded voice of Albert Miles, at any rate. "This is Albert. I'm not available right now. Please leave a message and I'll get back to you as soon as I can. Thank you, and have a wonderful day."

He cursed under his breath, thumbed the disconnect button on the receiver and pulled the door open simultaneously.

The phone dropped from his hand as he saw his visitor. It struck the ground and bounced before it slid into the corner.

Bob had never experienced fear before. Not real fear, at any rate. He'd never known that his life was about to be destroyed, that his world, so carefully crafted over the years, was about to crumble around him. He'd felt hatred many times, and he'd learned to appreciate love and even anxiety, but never once in his long existence as a demon or his short one among the human beings, had he ever truly known fear.

That changed when he saw the Hunter looking at him.

Forty-one years had passed since their last encounter and then the Hunter had been at a serious disadvantage. Crippled, bleeding, dying in front of his eyes, the Hunter had gone down in a screaming ball of fire while the entity that now called itself Robert Workham had managed a quick last-minute escape, jumping from the host body he had stolen and falling to the planet below.

This wasn't just the Hunter; it was the Hunter reborn. Oh, the face was the same, but younger, more vital. The body in perfect shape, the self-satisfied smile that had marked their first encounter had been gone the second and third time they met. Now, it was back, a shit-eating grin that promised nothing but misery.

Fear became a bright sun in the world of Bob Workham. The Hunter had found him.

His heart stuttered in his chest and the air that he'd been holding escaped from his mouth in a soft sigh of desperation. His eyes flew wide, bulging as his blood pressure soared and his knees nearly buckled beneath him.

Bob took two steps back and landed against the wall of the foyer, his hands clutched at his chest as if to stop his heart from bursting free and scurrying down the hall to find the closest hiding place.

Jonathan Crowley's face grew hard, but his eyes smiled behind the rimless spectacles he wore. Such an average face, it didn't seem possible that any expression there could generate the fear that assaulted Bob Workham.

And then Crowley made it worse. He stepped into Bob's house as if he owned the place and took four strides toward the rightful owner.

In the living room, Colleen and the kids watched their movie and Ariel broke into song. Amy sang along, her voice high, and clear, and sweet, and for once her brothers didn't even try to mock her.

Crowley opened his hand just below the level of his mouth and blew a light gray dust into the air. Rather than scatter itself across the ground, the powder soared in a straight line and then spread out, covering Bob from head to toe. The stuff was so fine it barely even irritated his skin.

"I. I. Oh God, I—" He couldn't make his mouth work. The words refused to come and even the very vowels that escaped past his lips were barely as strong as a dying man's last gasp.

Crowley lifted a finger to his lips and said "Shhhh. Wouldn't want the family to hear this, would we, Bob?"

He would have protested if he could have managed a breath.

"Been a long time, old sport." Crowley's words spilled past the sneer on his lean face. "Yessiree Bob. Long time."

He felt the tears that zinged through his eyelids, just below the threshold where they would have actually glistened in his eyes. Bob tried to breathe again, but he couldn't suck in enough air to make a difference.

Crowley leaned in as close as a lover, his lips almost brushing Bob's ear. "Come outside, Bob. I don't think you want your family to see any of this."

Crowley never took his eyes off of Bob as he slid backwards across the floor, his feet barely seeming to touch the ground. "Don't keep me waiting, Bobby. Go make your excuse and step outside."

"I—"

"Shhh. Save it for outside. Oh, and don't think of running. You run, and I take it out on them." Crowley finally looked away, just long enough to indicate the living room where the family watched an inane piece of fluff, unaware that Daddy was inches away from dying. The smile came back. That damnable smile the Hunter had worn the first time they'd met, when he cast Bob down into hell.

Crowley closed the door with a gentle touch, barely enough to make any sound at all.

Bob slid down the wall slowly, his legs no longer keeping up any pretense of strength.

Fear, unlike the other emotions he'd learned since walking among the humans, did not fade easily. It lingered in Bob's body and refused to be quiet.

He finally managed the strength to stand, and shook as he did so. Without a word to Colleen or anyone else, he reached into the closet and grabbed his thickest coat.

It was a hard thing to do, stepping through that doorway. It's always hard walking into what you know is your death.

Amelia stared at the house for a long time, and blinked only when she saw Crowley stepping across the threshold. He'd managed to slip past her, which really wasn't very surprising in the heavy snowfall.

A moment or two later, Jonathan stepped back outside and into the cold. She moved in his direction without conscious thought, going to him, drawn to him. She wanted so much to stop him from making a horrible mistake.

There was more to the story than simple revenge in Amelia's eyes. She wanted to keep Jonathan safe, of course, but she also wanted to keep the people in the house safe.

She just had no idea how to articulate that thought.

The snow was piling deeper and the day had not yet grown bright. The cloud cover kept the sun at bay and likely would for the duration of the storm, which didn't seem likely to end anytime soon. She stopped herself five feet away from Jonathan, who looked her way with an exasperated expression on his face.

"Hello, Jonathan."

"Is there a reason that you're spying on me, Amelia?"

"I'm not spying, Jonathan. I'm here to—"

"To stop me from doing naughty things?" That smile again, more of a snarl than anything else. He wondered sometimes why people got nervous when he smiled. It was because no matter how hard he tried to look pleasant, his bared teeth were a threat, a promise to bite into flesh and draw blood.

He hadn't been that way before his family was murdered. Maybe it had been his apparent age back then. He'd seemed calmer, more likely to be forgiving.

"Jonathan, you need to be sure. What you're thinking about…what you're planning to do, it can't be taken back, do you understand me?" She implored him with her words and took a few paces closer to him. The turmoil inside of him seethed and boiled. She marveled that the snow didn't melt beneath his feet.

"You don't even know what I'm planning, cupcake. You don't know shit." And there it was, the hatred again, directed at her. Oh, how he tried to hide it. Most times he succeeded to one level or another, but for now his rage was too great.

It broke her heart sometimes. Jonathan Crowley almost always did that.

"I'm not stupid, Jonathan. I'm not a little girl anymore." She tried to leave the hurt out of her voice, but if his expression said anything it was that she was failing.

"You called me and gave me the address, Amelia. And I appreciate that. But I was already on my way here. I already knew."

"How did you find out?"

"Not your concern."

"Don't be this way, Jonathan. Don't shut me out."

"That's not the way this works. I've told you before, we're not friends. We're never going to be friends."

"Yes, that's right. Jonathan Crowley doesn't need friends, does he? He's too big for that."

Jonathan's smile grew larger, sadistic. "Truth hurt? Tough. I'm here to do my business, to take care of something that's been bugging me for a while. Do us both a favor and walk away from it, Amelia."

"You're breaking the rules, Jonathan. No one asked you into this. You don't have any advantages."

"I've got all I need." He dismissed her that easily. He didn't even have to turn his back to do it. As far as he was concerned, she was no longer there.

And before she could do anything to change his mind, the door to the house opened again and a man stepped out into the bitter, cold landscape.

She knew his face. She'd studied it only a few hours ago. Robert Workham. He looked nice enough. A conservative's haircut and a pudgy body that she suspected was normally hidden behind a suit. Now he stood in the cold in jeans and boots, with a thick winter parka and a wool cap covering his ears.

And he, too, was a beacon. Jonathan Crowley fairly burned with hatred. Robert Workham reeked of fear.

Crowley stood perfectly still and looked at the man, his face calm and stony.

Workham looked back, his teeth worrying desperately at his lower lip.

"You're really him, aren't you?" Despite his fear, Workham's voice was calm.

"Who else would I be?" Jonathan's voice was a tight, thin line of noise: a scrape of nails across the inside of a wooden casket. His eyes, so unassuming under most circumstances, burned with their own intensity. With or without her empathic abilities, Amelia would have known exactly how furious the man was.

"How?"

"I don't die as easily as my family, Mr. Workham." Crowley grinned. "How about you? How long do you think you're going to last?"

"What about them?" Workham shook as he stepped forward. "What about my family?"

"What about *my* family!" Jonathan stepped across the snow, his feet seeming to float above the drifting white of the landscape. His voice broke then, a storm that had been suppressed for so very long and now was let loose.

"What about Elizabeth? What about Theresa? What about my little Jeremy? What about Wendy?"

Workham cringed as if slapped. "I'm sorry. Oh, please, I'm so very sorry."

"You ate their souls!" The air fairly shook and Crowley stepped forward and struck the man a savage backhand. Workham didn't fall; he soared backward and then crashed into the bushes near the front of his house. "You tore their bodies into bloody meat and ate their souls! How can you think you can ever apologize for that?"

The man crawled from the broken shrubs and looked over his shoulder, worried even now that his family might hear, or worse still, attempt to investigate.

"Tell you what, precious, you last long enough for me to get my satisfaction, and maybe I won't do to your wife what you did to mine. Maybe I won't make your little ones watch while she screams and begs. Maybe I won't make you watch."

Workham's face shifted through a dozen expressions of dread and fury before he finally managed to grow courageous. Whatever else the man was—and Amelia knew he was more than a mortal, could feel it in him—his love for the family he'd created was real.

"If you touch them..."

"What? You'll make me pay?" Crowley laughed. "You'll kill everyone I hold dear? That threat ring a bell with you? I remember when you said that the first time, Bobby Boy. I remember it well."

"I don't know what you want from me!" Workham's voice rose into a scream. "I can't make it right!"

"I want you to suffer." For just one moment the rage was gone, replaced by a low purr. Jonathan's eyes were half-lidded now, and the smile was back, that dreadful, frightful smile. "I don't want you dead, because that's not enough for me. Not anymore. I want you to suffer. I want you to have a taste of the pain you've put me through, Bobby, and I want to make sure you never, ever forget me again." The hatred returned. In all the time Amelia had known him, she'd seldom seen Jonathan angry enough to spit. His face looked inhuman, his posture, his gestures, nearly unholy.

"So kill me then, but leave them out of this, please!" Still on his knees, the man begged, his hands clasped together, his fingers pressed so tightly they were as pale as the surrounding snow.

Despite everything she did know, Amelia had no idea if Jonathan would be that kind.

They'd met four times.

The first time he encountered the Hunter, he'd been in Constantinople, released to wreak havoc on a man whose fortune was large enough to rule nations, and whose neighbor grew jealous not only of the wealth his neighbor possessed, but of the beauty of his wife.

For three days and nights he'd killed the man's family before the Hunter showed up and cast him down. Before he was banished he swore that he'd destroy everything the Hunter held sacred, everything he loved.

How many years did he suffer for his failure before he was summoned again and given a second chance? He couldn't recall. All he knew was that Paris was a fine place, indeed, and one where he was let loose for the sole purpose of destroying a prince who had grown fat on power and decadence.

Once he was done with his duty to the sorcerer who summoned him, he devoured the man's soul and began a reign of murders that should have been legendary.

And then the Hunter showed again: A different name, of course, but the same entity. They fought a second time and the arrogance of the Hunter! If he recognized the demon who'd sworn to destroy him, he never showed it.

The Hunter crushed him, shattered his body and sent him down into the unimaginable pain of imprisonment again.

And again he promised retribution.

The third time they met, he kept that promise. After being released from Hell again, he spent five years searching the world over. He finally found the name the Hunter used and then he found the people that the Hunter treasured.

The part of him he'd almost managed to contain still reveled in the blood and violence, the screams of the children were a sweet thing, the wife's agonies were unimaginable pleasures, but the desperate cries of the Hunter? Even now, that darkest part of him still shivered in ecstasy at the memory.

How many hours had he spent desecrating everything the Hunter held as sacred? Enough to ruin the man, to drive him to foolish gestures and empty threats. To leave the arrogant bastard weeping against the wall where he lay crucified, powerless and dying.

He remembered the Hunter's face, worn by age and streaked with tears of pain and fury. He remembered the old man letting him drive spikes through his wrists and legs, anything at all that he could do to stop the demon from hurting his family.

And that bit hurt, didn't it? He was facing the Hunter now, begging and desperate to save his family. He'd once trapped the Hunter and now he had become the hunted. He could have run and tried to save himself but that wasn't important any more. Anything he could do he would to save his family.

Just like the Hunter had, once upon a time.

It should have ended with the plane crash. He'd watched the Hunter's withered body break and burn and bleed until the heart must surely have stopped.

Somehow the man had come back again. He'd thought his vengeance complete, the source of his fears and hatred dead and gone forever.

The fear was a living thing inside of him, a hungry force that devoured his strength and fed on his desperation.

Once upon a time, when he was new to the mortal realms, Robert had done horrible, horrible things to the family of the man standing in front of him. He'd done them solely for revenge and without consideration of how his actions could come back to him.

He'd never known there could be so much to lose.

He stood slowly, his knees still threatening a rebellion with every inch he rose, and made himself face the Hunter. "Do it. Please, just get it done."

The man's eyes were locked on his and murderous. "Run."

"What?"

"I said run. Fifteen minutes. I'll be after you in fifteen minutes. Play to win, Bobby Boy. You let me catch you too easily and I promise I'll kill your family. I'll make them suffer, too; make what you did to Elizabeth seem like a fucking summer day picnic."

Robert ran.

His hands scrambled into his jeans and fished out the car keys. He knew all too well how dangerous the man was and he knew he'd need some sort of head start.

The car started easily despite the cold and he urged it carefully out of onto the road, gently easing his way over the snow and driving as meticulously as he could. Three minutes wasn't long, but he prayed it would be enough.

He didn't look back at the house. He didn't dare. He couldn't afford the time.

The car slewed down the road, fighting him the entire way, and he struggled to keep his course. In the end it was futile. The tires slid and the car shifted to the left and before he knew what was happening, the front end was crumpling into a light post. There was no way he'd get it moving again so he killed the engine.

Robert opened the door impatiently and willed the change he'd been trying to avoid. He'd hoped to have a surprise for the Hunter, a last chance to kill the man before he could be killed.

His skin throbbed and blinding pain ripped across his body. He fell to his knees again, a sudden heat burning his flesh and spasms convulsing his muscles.

The pain was wrong, not what he'd expected. Changing shapes was never easy, especially the sort of radical alterations he went through these days, but not like this. After several heartbeats, he stood back up and swayed drunkenly. His flesh was still human in form, his body unchanged.

"Oh, Hunter, what have you done to me?" He tried again to bring forth his infernal aspects and again he felt pain and little else.

And again, he ran, because in the end there was little else he could do…

"Why are you toying with him, Jonathan?" Her voice was so strained, so worried about him. Like she didn't have better things to do with her time.

"Same reason I stopped and took care of business before coming here, Amelia. I want this to last. I want to make sure he suffers, and I want to make sure I savor this. You only get one chance at revenge." He looked her way. "I don't want to fuck it up the same way he did."

And it was the truth for a change. He'd been frustrated when he had to stop and take care of Tim's dilemma, but the distraction had been good for him. It had given him time to simmer and contemplate exactly what he was going to do with his victim.

"You can't do this, Jonathan. There are rules; you're the one who always says so." And there she was, trying to be rational for him, trying to make him see the error of his ways.

"You're not getting it, Amelia, so let me spell it out. I don't fucking *care* about the rules right now. He's *mine*. I'm taking him down. I'm going to make him suffer and wish I'd be nice enough to kill him."

"But what if he kills you?"

"Not likely."

"He might not be as powerful, Jonathan, but without your abilities—"

"Still not getting it. Don't care." He looked at his watch, then looked at where the victim of his fury was standing next to his wrecked car. "I'd run faster than that, moron." He shook his head and rolled his shoulders, easing the tensions a bit. It wouldn't do to get too cocky, to let himself tense up. This wasn't going to be easy, but then, nothing worth doing ever was.

Amelia reached for him.

"Don't you dare touch me." His voice was a growl, and for once in her life she was smart enough to listen. "Not in the mood for sympathy, empathy or your damned concern right now. I'm in the mood to kill. Don't make me take it out on you."

He never looked at her. Instead, he watched Workham stumble and fall and get back up to keep running.

"Jonathan…"

He looked at his watch again.

"Gotta run, Amelia. You go ahead and watch if you want, you can even cheer Bobby on if that's your decision but if you try to interfere, I'll kill you."

Crowley started running, his feet pounding across the snow and never sinking more than a quarter of an inch into the whiteness.

Up ahead of him, the object of all his current passions stumbled again and barely managed to keep his footing. Workham's feet were sinking into the snow a good deal further and he was desperately trying to stay upright.

Crowley ran faster, Workham's fifteen-minute head start barely a fifth of the way finished.

Amelia watched him go and trembled. Maybe three minutes was all of the head start he intended to give. The man would be up to the fight or he would die quickly. Either way, Jonathan Crowley intended to have his satisfaction. It wasn't the cold that made her shiver; it was fear. Not for herself, not for Robert Workham, but for Jonathan Crowley. He was no longer rational, and that scared her a great deal.

Shaking her head, she followed him, watched from a distance and kept moving, determined to see the situation through to its conclusion. If she could help him, if she could *save* him, she would.

And if not? What then? She didn't know. She didn't want to think about it or imagine a world without him. He'd said more than once that there were others out there like him, others who would fight whatever came along. She knew he was right about that, too, because even when he'd vanished the world hadn't ended. Even when he'd stopped trying, the world had survived. Still, she didn't much like the idea of a world without Jonathan Crowley. She hated the notion.

The snow kept falling, obscuring her view, but she moved on anyway, doing her best to keep track of the Hunter and his prey.

Within four minutes, she'd lost hunter and hunted to the storm.

Amelia stood in the growing cold and thought very carefully about what she wanted to do to save him from himself.

The idea came to her easily enough, but getting the courage to actually do anything about it, that was more challenging.

Finally, she turned and headed back toward the Workham house, trying to ignore the fear that chewed at her insides.

Jonathan would be so very angry.

Bob ran as best he could, his skin still aching from his attempts to change. He looked behind him as often as he dared and never saw a sign that Crowley was on his trail, but he knew better from past experiences.

After he'd killed the man's family he left the area immediately. He drove to San Francisco and took his time putting his affairs in order.

Three weeks later, he'd taken a plane to the East Coast, ready to start a new life, in a new place. Back in those days you didn't need to bother with identification as long as you had the money and he'd managed to gather plenty of that. The one thing you could count on was that humans would hoard their money. Use the right words, the right promises and threats, and the money was an easy thing to acquire. He'd gotten plenty simply by killing the right people and being less flamboyant in his efforts. He grew wiser; he hid the bodies.

He left the Hunter behind, a broken wreck of a man, literally nailed to the wall and bleeding to death. He'd toyed with finishing the job, but there was no hurry. The old man was a broken waste of flesh. He'd suffer for a few days and then he would die.

But there was a chance the man would manage to recover. He could sense that simple truth, even past the blood and the smell of decay. In the long run Bob knew that was his real reason for moving, because he knew there was a chance the man would find him; a small risk, true, but still a real one.

He'd paid for a good seat near the front of the small plane and when he was properly situated, he sat and sipped a glass of wine. He'd been relaxing when the Hunter found him again. Crowley came from the back of the plane, limped through the door separating the compartments, speaking in a weak, ruined voice, speaking the words that would cast him down again.

He still remembered the pain, the unbearable agony of the words and how quickly he'd responded.

Weak did not explain the Hunter's condition. Devastated came closer and near death came closest. The face and name he wore then had been different, but Bob still held the memories and Bob attacked, his body effortlessly reverting to its true form, a killing machine that shamed the most dangerous natural animals in the world. His claws tore flesh, his fingers broke bones, his teeth crunched through layers of living being with ease, and the Hunter kept trying until the very end when the plane went down.

He could not be alive. That was the one prevalent thought that haunted Bob as he ran. The Hunter could not have survived the crash. No one, nothing had survived.

The snowstorm had grown worse still, and Bob shook the memories away as he cut across a parking lot that looked like a remnant from a distant ice age. He could see cars in the lot and the building itself, but the day was dark enough that the streetlights had activated and the glare that filled the air was enough to make him look down.

His feet were numb and his chest hurt from gulping down the frigid temperatures. His nose was running and his legs ached. To make matters worse, he was almost certain that he was lost. Nothing looked right and he'd probably left his neighborhood a while back.

He paused for a moment to catch his breath and reassess his location.

The fist that struck him in his stomach came out of the snow without warning. Bob felt himself lifted from the ground as the air was forced from his body. He fell again into the wintry mix and coughed violently as he tried to regain his breath.

Crowley helped him to his feet and when he was standing, hit him in the face hard enough to split his lip and rattle his teeth in their sockets.

While he tried to convince his muscles to move, the Hunter spoke to him. "What happens to the souls you eat? Do they stay with you? Do you send them down to hell for your masters?"

"I don't know..."

"Wrong answer!" Crowley's foot connected with the side of his head and sent him back into the cushioning white snow.

He thought the man would beat him to death then and there, but instead he backed away, shaking his head and scowling.

Finally Bob stood back up. "I never studied the process, Hunter. I never wanted to know. I ate them, that's all."

Before he could catch another breath, the man struck again, a blow into the nerve cluster under his arm that left the right side of his body aching and useless. And again, a brutal punch to the sternum that was just hard enough to avoid breaking the cartilage shield around his heart. After that Bob lost the ability to think for a while. He fell back into the bitter cold of the snow and felt nothing at all as the darkness claimed him.

He woke only a few moments later as Crowley dragged him along by his leg. His face was buried in the deepening snow and his nose felt like it had been sanded off. He sputtered and kicked as panic set in and Crowley dropped his leg.

The sky had actually grown darker, the storm worsening instead of getting better, and while the voice told him it was the Hunter standing above him, he could only barely make out the man's face.

"Good. You're awake. Now we can settle this."

His body ached in a hundred places and the only spots that didn't hurt were the ones that felt half-frozen.

"Why haven't you killed me yet?" The thought should have been comforting, it should have told him that there was a way out of his dilemma, but instead his stomach seized with fear again.

"I'm not done with you yet. I'm not satisfied." The man shrugged his shoulders, dislodging some of the snow that was covering the top of his overcoat and the top of his hair. He'd removed his glasses, but Bob didn't doubt for a moment that his adversary could see him in perfect detail.

"What are you going to do?"

"I'm going to kill you. I just haven't decided how yet."

Bob tried to change again and grunted as the pain washed through him again.

Crowley chuckled, tiny plumes of steam escaping from his mouth with each tiny laugh. "Like that? I didn't know for sure if it would work."

"What did you do to me?"

"Binding spell. You can't let out the demon inside of you, asshole, because I made sure it can't get away."

Bob shook his head and almost cried. All the time he'd spent trying to make sure that he could be as human as possible, sacrificing a great deal of the power that would have made this fight easier, and he'd never once considered a simple binding spell. A good one, done by someone of power, would have insured him his body for all time.

"I have money." There was no way the man would go for it, but he had to try.

"So do I. Money is one thing I never have to worry about."

Bob sat up, but didn't try to stand. His head was spinning too much for that. "I thought you'd say something like that."

"Do you love your family, Bobby Boy?"

He didn't have to think about it. "Yes. They're everything to me."

"Tell you what. I could let you live and kill them, how does that sound?"

"No." What else could he say? Life without them would be misery.

"It's what I should do. It's what you did to me." The Hunter's voice was toneless, without inflection. Bob would have preferred him yelling and ranting again.

"You won't."

"You so sure about that?"

"You protect people."

"No, I hunt monsters. Don't get confused about that."

Bob decided to try standing. He'd made it to his knees before Crowley knocked him back down with a foot planted in his chest. The blow to his sternum earlier flared into painful warmth.

"Don't get up on my account."

He groaned in pain and slowly rolled back into a sitting position.

"I keep telling people I've gotten soft." Crowley's voice was calmer, his shadowy face almost serene.

"Well, don't let me stop you."

"Funny man."

"Are you going to kill my family?"

"Have they been ripping people apart and swallowing their souls?"

"No! They're human."

"Then I probably won't have to kill them. They'll suffer enough when you're gone." Still he spoke without his voice rising or falling, a flat, toneless voice that was almost worse than the screaming had been earlier. It seemed too much like the calm before the storm.

"What do you mean?"

"You don't really think I'm going to leave your body around, do you?" The man sounded amused by the very notion. "Believe me, they'll never find any part of you. Your wife, what's her name?"

"Colleen."

"Colleen will worry about you for a long time. Seven or so years from now, she'll have you declared legally dead and everything that you own will go to her. Your children will wake up and find that Daddy has vanished. They'll never see you again. Oh, they'll think of you, but after a while they'll move on. Colleen might find somebody else. Good body, nice face. Barely looks like she's had three kids. I'm guessing she works out. I saw her through the window. She's lovely."

The panic came back. Colleen was his wife, his love, and the idea of her miserable was bad, but the thought of another man caressing her body was worse.

Crowley smiled. "Maybe I'll wait a year or so and then ask her out myself, but me or anyone else has to be better than what she got saddled with."

"Screw you."

"No thanks, cupcake."

They stood in silence for a few moments, both of them gathering their thoughts. Finally, Bob shook his head. "Just kill me and be done with it, Hunter. I don't much feel like freezing to death."

A cell phone rang in Crowley's pocket. He looked at Bob and shook his head. "Hold on, sport. Think about other ways to stop me. I should take this."

Bob shook his head and did his best to recover his strength.

He opened his phone and spoke into the device, but his eyes never left Bob. "Crowley."

"H-hello? Is this…Are you Jonathan Crowley?" The woman's voice was nervous.

"That's me. What can I do for you?"

"Mr. Crowley, I understand that you hunt monsters."

"That's one way to put it." He was beginning to think he was dealing with a crank call. Just in case, he started envisioning new and painful ways to torture the caller.

"I understand I have to ask you for your help, is that correct?"

He looked at the caller ID, but the number was unlisted.

"Yes, that's correct."

"Mister Crowley, I've been told that there's a monster currently hunting down my husband." The woman's voice broke. "I need to ask for your help in stopping the monster."

"What's your name?"

"My name is Colleen Workham, Mister Crowley. Please save my husband." Her voice degenerated into tears.

Crowley pulled away from the cell phone and stared at the screen as if it might give him answers.

"Nice one, Amelia. Very nice. Point taken." His voice was a low rasp.

When he spoke into the phone again, his voice was much livelier.

"You're in luck, Mrs. Workham. I have your husband right here. Alive and well. Would you like to say any last words to him before he dies?"

Workham looked up at him and shook his head.

The woman's sobs were clear to him even from a foot away from his ear and past the growing winds of the snowstorm.

"Don't you do this to me, Hunter!" Dear old Bob's eyes were wide and streaming tears. A slow smile teased the edges of Crowley's lips. He forced it back.

"You want to say your last goodbyes to your wife? Maybe explain to her why I'm going to kill you?"

Workham's face pinched into a miserable expression and his mouth opened and closed as he looked toward the cell phone.

Crowley smiled. "Last chance to talk to the woman you married. That's more than you gave me, you fuck." It was all bluff and bluster, but he hid it well. Jonathan Crowley could be a sadistic bastard and he knew it, but he normally reserved the torture sessions for the ones who had them coming. Colleen Workham and her children did not, to his knowledge, deserve to suffer what they were about to endure. He knew from firsthand experience. He'd lived through four decades of the pain. Thinking about the innocents, that was why Amelia had the woman call him. It was a weak point for Crowley. He didn't like to make people suffer, not unless they deserved it.

Crowley tossed his phone to Workham and crossed his arms. Bobby boy caught the phone and put it to his mouth and ear.

"Colleen? Honey?" The man shook his head. "No, babe. No. I'm not coming home." The tears fell fast from his face, and dripped from his quivering chin. "I…I did some bad things before we met. Now I have to pay for them. No. It's not the sort of situation where I'm going to need a lawyer." His face was so human, so very sincere. The tears he cried were real and the sorrow in his every word was deep and haunting.

Workham's shoulders shook and his face lowered until he was almost level with the snowy ground.

Crowley watched him and felt the rage. Amelia was trying to do the right thing again. She wanted to let him see the humanity that had developed in Robert Workham.

It didn't work. All he saw was Elizabeth screaming, bleeding, dying.

He tuned out the conversation. If he did listen, he might actually feel guilt.

He wasn't going to allow himself that luxury.

Robert Workham held the phone away from his body, extended as far as he could push it in an effort to avoid hearing his wife's pleas for him to speak to her.

Crowley stared down at him for a long while, watched him push his face into the snow and sob with loss. With heartbreak.

Crowley reached down and took the phone from Workham's hand. He listened to Colleen Workham's desperate voice for a moment and then killed the call.

He waited until Workham had cried himself out, a process that took longer than he'd honestly expected.

And when the man looked up at him, Jonathan Crowley struck a killing blow to Bob Workham's skull.

He waited for several more minutes as the storm raged, and then he got to work.

Despite all that he knew about the universe and the supernatural, there were still plenty of mysteries that he did not understand. One of them was what happened to the souls of people eaten by demons. It was rare to see a ghost in the first place, but in all of his time he'd never encountered the spirit of someone who'd run across a hungry demon. Not once.

He spoke words of power that had never been uttered within the continental United States, words that had last been spoken when Babylon was young. He wove his words carefully and cast the spells required to let him work in peace, without interruption by nature or man or beast from another world.

The storm faded to nothing around him, the snow and wind held at bay by his sorceries, and when he was ready, Jonathan Crowley got to work.

It's been speculated that the soul, the life force, the consciousness of a human being has neither weight nor mass, assuming it even exists.

Jonathan Crowley was not there to dispute the arguments for or against the soul's existence, nor was he planning to share what he learned with the world at large.

He had seen amazing things since he first walked the world. Had seen more since his family was murdered than most people could comprehend. He had dealt with ghosts and demons and far stranger things, but now the search was personal.

Robert Workham swore he didn't know what happened to the souls that he devoured. Jonathan Crowley didn't know either, but he intended to find out.

And because he had waited for so very long, and because he wanted to know that Workham and the demon inside him suffered for a very long time, he cast an additional curse into the blend. He made sure the dead man felt everything he did to him and he took his time.

Amelia Dunlow stared at the nighttime sky and waited. The storm had done its worst and dropped a good deal of snow, but the plows were already at work, clearing the main roads. They were in Chicago, after all, and the town knew how to handle an occasional blizzard. The air was, if anything, colder than before, but still she waited, fully exposed to the elements. The chauffeur she'd hired was sound asleep behind the wheel of the luxury limousine. He'd been asleep for quite some time.

Not far away, the Workham house sat in the darkness, silent and alone. The people inside were sleeping. She did that much for them at least. Or maybe for herself. Feeling their grief had been a painful burden. Her own loss was still fresh and vivid and might be worse soon if Jonathan managed to fail in his endeavors, or even if he succeeded. Better to let them rest until she was gone and could avoid the sensations that came from the place.

Jonathan Crowley had not yet returned. His car sat only a short distance away, unmoving and half buried in the snow.

A very light crunch of footsteps in snow let her know that Jonathan was closing in on her even before she felt him. The anger was still there, but cooler now, less like a pending disaster.

She turned to face him and he held out a large Starbucks cup of coffee. "Took a while to find one that was open."

She took the cup and stared at him. He didn't look away. His eyes issued the same challenge as before, the same warning.

"Did you kill him?"

"Of course I did." He shrugged. "I told you I would."

"What about his family?"

He looked away from her and stared at the house for a while before talking. "What about them?"

"Do you plan on doing anything to them?"

"No." He shook his head. "Well, yes. I'm going to cast a spell to make them forget my name. Shame on you." The chastisement was small. It could have been much worse, would have been, she suspected, if she had succeeded in her plans to thwart him. "They never did anything to me. Of course, if they try to bring him back, that's a different story."

"How can you be so cold, Jonathan?"

"You have to ask?" He looked back at her and stared hard. This time, for a change, she didn't look away.

"You're not, Jonathan. You're not that cold."

"You'd be surprised."

"Liar."

He saluted her with his cup of coffee and then took a deep drink from it.

"What did you do with him? Why were you gone so long?"

"Do you ever stop asking questions?" the edge of exasperation was back in his voice.

"No. Not until you answer them."

"That's called being a pain in the ass, Amelia. You should try to avoid it. It makes people feel negatively toward you." Sarcasm again, his resort whenever anything came too close to being personal.

"But, will there be consequences?" Jonathan Crowley was a very powerful entity. Sometimes she had trouble even thinking of him as human. He could manifest amazing powers as long as he was performing the duties he had taken on. But there was a check and balance system in place, one that she had never fully understood. Sometimes when he stepped outside of the rules, bad things happened to Jonathan Crowley. Not fatal things, but bad.

"I didn't use those abilities, Amelia. I didn't have to. He was weak." He shook his head, disgusted by the suggestion.

She nodded and flashed an apologetic smile. She couldn't help it. She worried. Amelia swallowed and went ahead with her interrogation. "What did you find out?"

"About what?"

"About your family. What did he do with their spirits?"

Jonathan looked away. His lips pulled into a scowl and then down into a frown. It was seldom that anyone saw him looking unsure of himself.

"Jonathan?" She got foolish and reached out for him with one hand. He stepped back and shook his head, his eyes casting a warning.

"I don't know. I don't know what happened to them. I know he killed them and stole their souls. Beyond that, anything is possible." She caught the images that came from him, felt his frustration. He'd performed dark rituals indeed as he destroyed all traces of Robert Workham's body. He'd carefully sifted his fingers through the dead man's form, pulling and separating meat from spirit and then sorting the demonic essences from the human energies. There had been spirits locked within the man, captured within the fibers of his being that were likely the undigested remains of whatever souls he had consumed.

She felt his frustration as she caught the images in her mind. Crowley's hands searching, his desperation growing as he searched for any possible hint of his wife or his children among the captured and destroyed.

With even a shred of their life force, he could have, perhaps, set them free from whatever pains they suffered. Or even, possibly, have said his goodbyes to them once and for all.

"I looked, Amelia. I looked everywhere and freed so many, but they weren't there. None of them. Not even a hint they'd ever been there."

That calm surface broke again and this time it was grief that emanated from him, pain and loss washed from Jonathan Crowley as surely as his rage had bathed her earlier.

"Jonathan, I'm so sorry."

The coffee was dropped to the ground as she moved forward and put her arms around his waist, locking herself into an embrace that he resisted. His hands stayed low and at his sides as he looked away from her, but this time he did not push her aside. That was something, at least.

Finally, Amelia felt his arms move up and pull her in closer. She hugged him fiercely and wept again, her own sorrow still fresh, the pain from the sleeping family still present and now the emotions that Jonathan tried so hard to never show. All of them combined to make her feel both alive and vulnerable as she wept.

She nestled her face against his neck and collar and felt the warmth of her own breath as she held him.

A momentary foolishness, really, an old desire that returned at the worst times. Amelia leaned her head up until her lips could meet his and kissed him.

For the first time in her life, Jonathan kissed her back. His hands on her waist pulled her closer for a moment and her heart beat at twice the usual speed at the thrill of contact. For one brief moment, she made contact with him, felt his desires and passions as his lips responded.

And then he broke the kiss, his eyes half-lidded as he looked at her. The grief, the anger, the pain were all gone again, locked away behind whatever barriers Jonathan Crowley had around his heart. He hid himself from her again and she stifled the urge to cry over the loss.

His eyes were cold and stern, but his voice was soft. "Bad girl. Very bad. Go home to Mike, Amelia. I'll visit you in a few days."

Amelia nodded silently and stepped away from him. Shame made her mute and kept her from looking at him.

A moment later she was climbing into the limousine and Jonathan was opening the driver's door and whispering something to the chauffeur.

She wasn't supposed to hear his promise to make the man suffer if he caused her any harm, but she heard it any way.

A moment later she was on her way back to the airport and Jonathan was watching her go.

There was nothing to be said, nothing she could do to make amends for kissing him. He would forgive her as he had in the past.

At least she hoped he would.

Crowley walked slowly to his car, feeling every year of his true age. He cast his spell and stole his name from Colleen Workham and her family, though he knew it would bring them no peace, no comfort.

He had known going in that there would be no real satisfaction in killing the demon in human form. Oh, there was a certain visceral delight, to be sure, but no deep and abiding satisfaction in a job well done.

He hadn't lied to Amelia. There was no trace of his family's spirits within the demon. All gone, bye-bye. Nothing. He'd felt the spirits of people dead for over a century inside the beast, not fully cognitive ghosts or displaced souls, but remnants. There were even a few that went back further than that, but of the Jonathan Crowley family, there was nothing.

Nothing, as if they'd never existed.

He might have believed it too, that he'd lost his fool mind once and for all, but he had pictures, he had evidence and he had memories of laughter and joy to see him through the darker times.

The car started without trouble and he patted the steering wheel affectionately. "Let's get out of here, okay? No games either. Stick to the road, because I'm really very tired."

The snow didn't stand a chance. The vehicle changed as it moved forward, regressing in years and growing larger until it finally settled on a vintage Thunderbird shape. The engine roared and then idled down a bit as the white walled tires moved forward with slow patience.

Jonathan Crowley barely noticed the road. Instead, he looked at the folded paper he took from his shirt pocket.

The paper was ragged and worn, folded several times more now than it had been when Albert Miles handed it to him. It was just a piece of paper really, but it held something inside it now, something dark and pained.

He reached over to the dashboard and pulled a small satchel from inside it. Within the cloth sack there were several crystals, none of them remarkable or particularly valuable.

Crowley chose a clear piece of quartz and cupped it in his hand, muttering the ancient words softly, as if there were a chance that anyone could hear them.

And when he was done he slipped the crystal into the hand holding the slip of paper and wrapped it tightly into a ball.

Three last words and the paper dissolved into ash. The ash in turn bled into the crystal as easily as ink into water. He watched the darkness swirl for a moment and finally settle into a pattern within the stone.

Souls, it has been said, have no weight, no mass. Maybe that was true, but the crystal felt heavier within his palm as he held it and studied the intricate spirals of darkness within it.

"I told you, I want you to suffer."

He slipped the crystal into his shirt and settled back to drive for a while.

It wasn't all that far back to Bolingbrook and the families he'd left there. He had a bit of unresolved business to take care of.

The house on Wickhaven Street was empty. A good neighbor had taken the time to board up the broken windows. He could have gone looking for Laura Daniels and found her, but in the long run he was done with her. She'd scarred her mind and her life and there was little he could do to make it better. Still, he'd have to check up on her eventually, if only to make certain she didn't try anything else foolish.

No taint of the demonic or ghostly remained in the house, so he moved on to the other place he had to visit.

The Merriweather were having dinner when he arrived. The family ate in silence, both of the men in the house looking mildly puzzled. They had no idea what had happened, most likely. Sarah wasn't the sort who liked to explain when something went wrong. He doubted that much would change.

But there was something he could do to make their lives a little easier, something he should have done four years earlier, would have done if he hadn't been in a foul mood.

It was a simple spell, but oh, so very powerful. He made them forget.

They would not forget Tim, and likely Erica would remember being haunted by him, because there's only so much a person can forget before he'd be forced to change her mind and personality and that wasn't on his agenda. But the memories would be distant, faded and, hopefully, would not leave her carrying the burdens of what had happened to her over the last four years.

Sarah would remember what she had done. He made sure of that. She would know better than to ignore anything else that came along and tried to pull a fast on one of her loved ones. He wanted her to have the guilt, the sure knowledge that she had hurt her child through a desire to be free of the supernatural.

What he made them forget was him. He no longer wanted to be remembered by them and wasn't quite sure why it had been important in the past. Like as not it had been infatuation. Sara had come close to being someone important. Closer than he liked to think about.

That was in the past, which was exactly where it belonged.

So he made them forget. As always, there were other aspects to the enchantment. Should the time come when something did arise, Sarah or Erica would pick up the phone and place a call. He'd answer it. And if they asked the right question, he'd come back again and do what he could to make things right. It was what he did. In the long run, it was all he had.

Ten minutes after he stopped at their home, Jonathan Crowley left the Merriweather and their small world behind. There were other things to do.

He drove toward Amelia's house, because he knew he needed to speak to her and because there were books that had to be taken care of.

Also, it was always nice to piss off Mikey whenever he had the chance. Mike Blake just begged to be abused and he was glad to accommodate.

Later, he might stop by Serenity Falls and check in on the people there. If Albert Miles had been visiting, anything was possible, and any chance to mess with Albert Miles was going to be a good thing in his book for as long as the other man existed.

The work crews were handling the main highways and driving back to the Dunlow place was relatively uneventful.

He paused once on the trip when the thoughts of Elizabeth and the children snuck up and hit him from behind. He had the rest area to himself and walked along the snowy parking lot for a while, breathing in the cold air and clutching a certain stained crystal in his hand.

Deep within the crystal, something tried desperately to move and could not. From time to time it screamed in pain and frustration, but no one aside from Crowley could hear it.

Robert Workham was dead. He had been ever since the demon took control of his body. What remained of his soul had been among the many released from imprisonment when he took the time to pick the demon apart.

The demon itself was his prisoner, weakened to near extinction and held within a cage it could never escape. Locked into a room where it could find no solace, no peace from its memories of a life filled with loved ones and success, a life freed from Hell.

Jonathan Crowley knew just the place on the shelves of his study where he would place the crystal. He would leave it there to keep him company on the nights when his misery felt like a weight that would surely crush him, and he would take great comfort from the stained quartz.

It seemed appropriate to him, and in the long run, that was all that mattered.

Home for the Holidays

'Twas the season.

The roads leading into town were nearly cleaned of the thick sheath of snow that had blanketed the area for the last week and there were Christmas lights in the windows of most of the houses and all of the shops. One elemental truth stood against any and all religious differences during the holiday season: Christmas decorations meant more customers. Even the very Scroogiest shop owners knew that simple fact, and all of them did their best to take advantage of it.

They'd have had the damnedest time when it came to Jonathan Crowley. He'd been known to celebrate the season on behalf of others a few times, but not in longer than most of the stores on Main Street had been around.

Black Stone Bay was a beautiful town and half deserted for the holidays. Two universities took up a good portion of the area and with school out of session most of the students had gone home, leaving the campuses oddly silent despite the festive decorations. It leant the town a haunted air, though he could easily sense there were other reasons for that sensation. No town of any age managed to stay free of dark spots, places where life had gone wrong or death had grown cancerous. Black Stone Bay was a town most places aspired to; the people were well off, the crime rate was light—with a few exceptions—and the town was postcard perfect. It had been years since he'd come through the area and remarkably little had changed since then. There were no new developments, no subdivisions that had grown into the location, or overshadowed older neighborhoods. No matter who might want to bring change to the town, the people who lived there would never tolerate the idea.

There was little space for the nouveau riche in the place. The old money families saw to that.

The very notion set Crowley's teeth on edge. He had no special love of the wealthy, or of the needy. He had no special love for people, if the truth must be known, but they called on him just the same, and with no consideration of what they asked when they made their requests.

"So, tell me about your friend." He looked at the latest in an endless line of people who'd asked for help. The woman was not a stranger. He'd met her twenty years earlier when she was in college herself and living in Los Angeles. Back then Laura Natchez Montgomery had planned to be the next big thing as an actress. Two decades had removed that desire and replaced it with a fairly large family, including a husband, three children and two dogs. Dreams change. Jonathan Crowley could have told her that when they met, but knew she wouldn't have listened. Most people don't want to hear unpleasant or inconvenient truths when they're young and still know everything.

Laura sighed and looked out the window while she composed herself and tried to figure out exactly what to say. She was not a previous client. He had never been asked to help her out of a dilemma, but he'd come to her assistance just the same. They met while he was on the hunt and tracking down a killer. A flesh eater if he remembered correctly, one that killed its victims and then let them rot for a few days before it picked the bones clean. Laura had been unlucky enough to find one of the bodies and catch the damned thing's attention. She was a striking girl as he recalled, and the thing that had run across her agreed. It was a matter of timing really, blind luck that kept her from being raped by the nightmare. It was just tearing her clothes away, cackling as she screamed and tried to fight it off.

For Crowley it had also been a perfect distraction to let him take the damned thing down once and for all. The seams on Laura's jeans split open and she cried out at exactly the same time he was driving a ceremonial sword into the back of the demon's skull. The impact had broken the blade, much to his disgust. He hadn't been able to find a replacement and it wasn't for lack of looking over the years.

As he often did, he made sure she forgot about his existence and what had been done to her, with the simple added command that she would remember him and how to contact him should she run across another situation where he might be useful.

Two decades later she called him about a friend of the family.

"I still can't get over how little you've changed..." Her voice drifted sleepily. He hadn't changed. She had. Two decades weighed on her, etching fine lines in her features and transforming her from a tiny sexpot into a mother of three with the hips to prove it. Crowley looked exactly the same. The only noticeable difference was likely in his clothes and that was just because it was a damned site colder in New England at Christmastime than it was in California at the height of the summer.

"That's not why we're here, Laura. You wanted to tell me about your husband's friend." He allowed himself a small flash of a smile and waited while she thought over the situation.

Her eyes traveled along the length of him, not ogling, but absorbing. He was not normal and sometimes it took people a while to adjust to that fact. He was tolerant. Well, at least for the moment. The silences were stretching his willingness to behave himself.

"He's not..." She sighed. "He's not my husband's friend. He's my uncle. I just, I didn't know if you would take me seriously if I said he was a family member."

His lips pressed together and he forced himself to remain pleasant. He wasn't known for his patience, and liars, while amazingly common in his experience, almost always managed to piss him off.

"Oh, nothing to worry about. I don't need him to be anything to you one way or the other. I just need to know what the situation is that has me in Rhode Island instead of home for the holidays." He stared pointedly until she got the hint and nodded her head. He had nothing to go home to, but that wasn't any of her business and so he opted not to share the information.

"Turner is my uncle. My mother's brother, but a lot younger than her. He's only around five years older than me. We have never been overly close, but we know each other, of course." She smiled apologetically and Crowley nodded his encouragement. For some people talking about family was like pulling teeth. "He lost his family a few years ago." She looked out the passenger's side window of his car as he moved slowly, smoothly down the road. "He was at work, and somebody broke in. Somebody killed all of them. His wife, his children." She sounded apologetic, as if she were responsible for the entire situation. He was always amazed by how many people seemed to worry about that.

The silence stretched again, until he shook his head. "We're almost there. You should give me the details. Hit the high points."

"Well, the murders, they changed him. Turner became sullen, withdrawn, not that anyone blamed him, of course. He got better when he remarried, that made a big difference. It was almost like he'd been sick for a long time and then recovered. I don't know. Maybe it's that some people just need to have family with them to be complete, you know?"

He nodded. He could remember what that was like.

"Anyway, last year everything started going south again. He was fine, his new wife, his new step kids, even the new baby on the way, everything seemed like it was perfect and then he just…he lost it."

The light on the road ahead turned red and Crowley slowed the car down and stopped. He turned to look at her. Her expression was one he'd grown far too familiar with over the years; she looked quietly, desperately stunned, as if she'd just survived an unexpected car wreck where she was fine and everyone else was mangled.

When she spoke again the words were rushed, as if getting them out quickly would make it easier somehow. "Turner was fine at Thanksgiving, and for a week after that, but then he started changing. He went from open and friendly and loving to quiet and angry. He wouldn't answer my calls, and his new wife, Holly, she stopped by three days before Christmas in tears. He was screaming all the time, losing his temper and finally he told her to get out of the house before things got worse. So we took her in, we kept her over the holidays and did what we could to make everything okay. And then three days after Christmas, Turner came around apologizing and said he'd just succumbed to the pressure from work. That he'd basically lost it but he was better."

The light changed and Crowley started driving again.

"He was fine." Her tone said it all. She couldn't understand how her uncle could go crazy and get better so fast, but she believed he had done just that. "It took almost four months before Holly forgave him, really forgave him, I mean. The baby's what made the difference. And Turner loves that little boy, you can see it, you know? Even if he'd had any sort of problems with Holly or her children, he loves that little baby."

He could see the house now; there was a tree in the front yard with glowing lights and decorations, an illuminated tribute to the birth of a demigod to some, and to others merely a sign of the time of year when most people seemed a little more tolerant of their neighbors. He looked her way and asked with his eyes if he had the right place and she nodded her answer. A moment later he was pulling over in front of the place and killing the engine.

Inside the house there were lights and decorations as well, but even knowing that a family lived there, the house felt empty, cored out and abandoned.

"Finish it. Tell me." He pushed his glasses up the bridge of his nose and stared hard at her.

"The baby, he started crying all the time about two weeks ago. I mean all the time. He wouldn't sleep, he wouldn't eat. He just screamed and cried like he was being tortured. And around the same time Turner started acting like he was acting last year."

Crowley nodded. "You think he's being haunted."

"Well, yes, I suppose I do."

"When did his family die?"

"It was right around Christmas time."

"His family, are they staying with you again?" he remembered the suitcases, and there had been a hint of baby powder in the air.

"Yes." She sounded just a little puzzled by his knowing.

"The baby. Did the baby stop crying when he got to your house?"

"How did you know that?" She didn't just sound surprised, she sounded suspicious.

"You called me, remember?" He stared hard at her, unflinching, until she looked down and nodded her head. "It's a good sign. It means whatever is affecting your uncle isn't following the rest of his family, it's just dealing with him."

That was true enough, but if there had been anything in her house when he came to see her he'd have noticed it.

"Of course. I'm sorry." Her voice was a whisper. He looked away from her and opened his door.

"Well, there it is and here we are. Let's see what we can do for your Uncle Turner, shall we?"

Laura nodded and they stepped out of the warmth of the car and into the harsh cold wind. She was bundled into a thick fur coat that probably cost as much as her maid earned in a year. The wealth was something she took for granted, which meant she had changed a great deal from when she was a teenager. She was happy, deep inside where it counted, she was pleased with her world. Crowley envied her that.

He'd spent fifteen minutes inside her home and taken in all of the details he needed. In addition to the signs of visitors, he'd seen pictures of the woman and her husband, her kids. Three children, two daughters and a son, and didn't that put an ache in his heart? Didn't that bring back a special twist of pain when he remembered his past and the family he'd had? Oh, yes, my yes, it most certainly did. The family room had been rearranged to accommodate a massive Christmas tree that already had an explosion of gifts under it. Packages wrapped in every imaginable color and festooned with ribbons and bows. He looked away before he could let himself stare too openly.

There was no time for sentimentality and really, no desire. The past was best left behind.

A smile played around his mouth as he looked at the house Laura had directed him to. "Mostly. Mostly the past is best left behind." He stepped onto the walkway, not as clean as it could have been and in need of repairs, he noted. "There are always exceptions."

"I'm sorry?" Laura hadn't heard his words clearly. That was all right, too. They weren't meant for her.

"Nothing to worry yourself about," he waved a hand to dismiss her query. "Why don't you introduce me to your friend so we can get this over with?"

Laura didn't question him. Few people did. Most seemed to understand on an instinctive level that letting him have his way was the quickest method of getting him to leave, and even the people who wanted his help seldom wanted him around for long.

She walked up to the door and knocked briskly, her gloved knuckles rapping the wood hard enough to make her presence known to anyone around.

Almost a minute later the door opened and a young woman peered out: she was either a hooker—unlikely—or hired help. Crowley stared only long enough to acknowledge that she was the maid. He ignored the conversation between Laura and the woman and instead looked around the outside of the house. A nice place, not overwhelmingly fine, but better than average. There was a darkness around the place, however, that made perfect sense to Crowley. Something was wrong. Something had invited itself into the house and made itself comfortable.

He opened his senses, did his best to find the source of the discomfort, but that was too easy and whatever was there didn't want to be seen. Not by him, at least.

Laura looked in his direction and smiled patiently. She was waiting on him while he was off daydreaming. Sloppy. He needed to remember why he was here. He apologized with a smile of his own and moved forward into the home of a man he had never met.

Once past the threshold he felt them, the spirits of the house, the entities that filled the place and held sway over the head of the household. They were hidden, but they were not quiet. They howled their outrage and cursed the man's existence with malignant fury.

He noticed the sounds. Laura walked on as if there were nothing at all to be afraid of, and if he was right, there was no reason at all for her to be worried.

She wasn't the target.

The maid looked toward Crowley and smiled apologetically. "Mr. Hamilton, he's not himself lately."

"That's why I'm here, isn't it? To get him back to himself?"

"Oh, are you a doctor?" She was cute and he resisted a dozen different comments he could have made in response. Instead, he just nodded. He hadn't expected a maid. The house wasn't really large enough to leave a reason for him to expect a maid and he doubted the man could afford the luxury for his wife.

"Turner?" Laura's voice rang out harshly enough to startle the maid. Crowley simply pressed his lips together.

The man came out of a doorway to the left. His eyes were wide and surprised, his face pale and puffy. His features bore a strong resemblance to the woman who'd called on Crowley in the first place, but stress had aged him more than the five years that separated them, and the haunted expression ruined any illusion of happiness and contentment.

Laura opened her mouth to speak, and Crowley held out a hand to silence her. He stepped past her and closer to her uncle.

"You aren't having a good time of things lately, are you?"

"Who are you?"

"I'm a specialist. Your niece told me you need help and that's what I'm here to take care of."

The man shot an angry look at Laura that was completely out of place for what she had done. Crowley noticed it, but said nothing.

"I don't need a specialist. I need to be left alone."

"Sure. That's why your wife and your kid are over at Laura's place, because everything is just fine."

"How dare you?" Like so many people, he was surprised when someone stated the obvious. Manners were a good thing in small doses, but did remarkably little for Crowley's peace of mind.

"It's Christmas Eve and I'm here instead of at home." He crossed his arms over his chest and looked at the man over the rim of his glasses. The smile that slipped across his mouth was cold and predatory and Turner blanched a bit. "That's pretty much all the reason I need to dare anything, sport."

"Listen, this is my house." The expression said it all. He was angry, and that was expected, but he was also worried about something. Not Crowley. He hadn't even begun to give the man a reason to be afraid. It was something else, and Crowley struck at that particular nerve quickly.

"Yeah, I get that. But it's not your house. Not really. If it was your house, you wouldn't have to send your family away to keep them safe, would you?"

The eyes widened. A sign that he'd struck the nerve he'd aimed for.

"Listen, Laura, I want you and this lovely young lady to go to the kitchen for a minute, okay? I need to talk to Turner alone."

Laura opened her mouth to say something and snapped it shut just as quickly when she saw Crowley's expression. Instead, she nodded and all but pushed the girl out of the room. Crowley kept his eyes on them until they were safely away from the master of the house.

"Listen carefully. I really don't want to be here. Your house has a serious shadow on it. I need to know who is haunting you." He spoke quickly and quietly, knowing fully that the answer he got would be a lie.

"No one. I don't even know what you're talking about."

Crowley's smile bloomed, a dark and venomous expression. He had to resist a sudden urge to laugh.

"Listen to me very carefully. You want to tell me the truth, because I can help you. I can make them go away, but I need to know what I'm dealing with and why they're hovering around you."

The room grew colder as he spoke, and Crowley, who was used to dealing with dead things and not the least bit surprised by the change, watched Turner flinch as surely as if he'd been slapped across the face.

"You should leave. Take Laura with you." Turner's voice was trying for calm and failing miserably. His eyes looked around with a quiet desperation, but saw nothing.

The air temperature dropped substantially for the second time and the man stepped away from the threshold he'd been standing in and retreated back into the room he'd come from.

Crowley followed and chuckled. "Seriously, you've got a bad case of the holiday spooks. Tell me who it is before things get worse."

They'd entered the dining room, which was set up with a small feast. The meal was laid out, a spread worthy of a dozen people, complete with settings, opened bottles of wine, eggnog, a ham and a turkey with all of the fixings.

"You have to leave. They want to eat now." The man's voice was hollow, weak. He swallowed, his face paler than before, his skin sweating profusely despite the frigid temperature in the room. Every breath, every word he uttered sent small plumes of condensation past his lips.

They tried to hide themselves from him but Crowley forced the issue. His hand reached into the thick winter coat he sported and sorted past several stones and two small bags of salt until he found the cellophane strip twisted around a pinch of grave mold mixed with sulfur and ash. A quick utterance, no more than a dozen mumbled words and then the fine black grit in the palm of his hand lifted into the air and dispersed evenly through the room. The cloud of dust settled itself, seemed to stick to the air around Turner. It layered itself in a thin mist and revealed the shapes that did their best to avoid being seen.

Two women stood in the room and near them, like satellites around twin moons, a half dozen children circled. Turner stared, his eyes bugging wider than Crowley would have thought possible.

"What? You haven't seen them before?" He let the humor creep into his tones. He didn't know exactly what the man in front of him had done, but he suspected Turner was responsible for the spirits that surrounded him.

Crowley let himself smile and scratched at his left hand.

"I-I-How did you do that? Why are there so many of them? I only wanted Michelle..." He tried to look everywhere at once, at all of the shapes and the faces hinted at by the black powder draped across their translucent forms. Apparently it was simply too much for him. Turner sat down abruptly at the head of the table, his face a study in misery.

The smile was wrong so he killed it. Made himself look stern. "Did you kill them, Turner? Or did you just miss them too much? They look mighty pissed off, whatever the case." He quickly scanned the room and frowned; it was getting colder and more than that, there seemed to be more of the shapes than he remembered.

"You wouldn't understand." Turner hid his face in his hands, mumbling the words past his clasping fingers.

"What's there to understand? You missed them, so you called them back. You think you're the first person to ever summon a dead loved one or two from the other side of death?" Crowley stepped closer, pushing his way through a dead boy who simply dispersed, leaving a thin black powder across the floor in his wake. "You think you're the only one who's ever wanted another chance at happiness?" The rage snuck in as he spoke, stoking the fury that always waited just under the surface of the Hunter's calm demeanor.

"I just wanted them back to say goodbye. I didn't expect them to keep coming back." He kept his hands over his face, and Crowley, who had been moving closer, felt the fine hairs on his neck rise and stepped back. You fight enough things in darkness and on unfamiliar territory you learn to trust your instincts.

"How long have they been after you?" He could hear the women coming back, their steps tentative, uncertain if they should enter the room. The shadowy forms all around them—enough now to crowd a bus station: there were more shapes coming from somewhere, and not all of them could be his family—looked toward the doors with unsettling hunger on their hollow faces.

"It's been five years. Just at Christmas at first, but then they started coming for longer stays. I couldn't hide them anymore; Holly was starting to ask questions and the kids... sometimes they could see them." He looked at Crowley with a trembling lower lip. "Do you understand? They could see the dead people."

"What? You thought they were your special entertainment?" Crowley's mouth curled into a scowl of disapproval. "They're dead, you damned fool. They're supposed to stay that way."

He saw the movement, the slight push at the door, and heard Laura's voice. "Is it okay to come in now?"

"No! No, Laura Keep away from here!" For the first time Turner seemed genuinely scared. He rose from his seat, his arms reaching as if to block her actions from across the room.

Crowley was faster. He pushed the door shut violently enough to shake the wall. Laura let out a squawk on the other side of the barrier, shocked by the sudden action. "Is everything okay in there?" Her voice had risen at least an octave and her stress was apparent.

Crowley smiled, though there was nothing kind about the expression. "You really screwed the pooch, didn't you? They're here for more than a holiday meal, aren't they?"

"They always come for Christmas dinner; I can't get rid of them." He looked at the shapes that moved, surging into the room from somewhere beyond the physical plane. Crowley looked carefully and finally saw the rift, understood what was happening.

"Oh, you damned fool. There's always a cost, isn't there?" He'd have to check. He'd ask Laura on the way back to her house, before he wiped the memories of the night from her head.

"They wanted...They wanted my family. Again." Turner's voice broke at last and he shook his head. "I couldn't give them Holly or the kids. I already lost one family!"

There had been two women present among the first spirits, and several children besides.

"How many times have you been married, you son of a bitch?" The words were cold, distant. Any sympathy he might have had for the man he was supposed to save was gone.

"Three times, okay? I wanted my family back, is that so wrong?" He was pleading, as if there was a chance that Crowley would somehow find it in himself to grant absolution.

"Last year your family left and you called for someone to cook for you. That's how this works, isn't it? You have to offer up someone, somebody to pay the price for letting them back in, or sending them away." He stared at the man, stunned. "You've done this before."

"I had no choice!" Oh, he was crying now, showing his misery for Crowley, showing how he'd suffered for the last few years.

"Was it this bad last year?" His was almost yelling to be heard over the hissed murmurs of the dead.

"It was never this bad before." Turner's voice was barely audible over the sound of the dead.

"Here's a secret for you, Turner, old son. The Dead don't like being where they are. It's cold and lonely. Here, this place? It's a lot happier for them."

"I can't make them go away. I've tried!"

"What rituals did you use?" There were always methods for reversing a spell, but he had to know which incantation had been used in the first place if he was going to make this painless.

Turner did the one thing guaranteed to anger Crowley. He lied. "I don't remember. I don't have the book anymore."

There were times when Jonathan Crowley was too nice for his own good and times when he was too lenient as far as he was concerned. He looked at the man in front of him, surrounded by the dead who demanded sacrifices, and knew that there was never going to be an easy fix for the situation. Given the opportunity, Turner Harrison would do it again. He did not want to learn from his mistakes. He simply wanted to have everything turn out his way, regardless of the cost.

"Fair enough. Handle your own problems, Mr. Harrison."

"What?" Oh, that got him thinking, didn't it? Suddenly there was more to consider.

"I said handle it yourself!" Crowley left the room, pushing the door open in a hurry and almost knocking Laura on her ass in the process. The atmosphere was quieter on this side of the door, the air warmer, less turbulent.

"Mr. Crowley, where's Turner?"

"He's staying here. We're not." He didn't give her a chance to argue, but instead grabbed Laura by her bicep and led her toward the front door. The maid hesitated for a second and then started following. He looked over his shoulder at her and nodded. "This is the part where we want to run."

Laura tried to resist but he was far too strong for her. He lifted the woman in his arms and ignored her frantic attempts to hit him, to make him let go. She started to say something but the sudden screams from the dining room dwarfed whatever words she tried to speak.

Crowley didn't stop to listen, much as part of him wanted to. Instead, he forced the front door open and when she got feisty a second time he physically hurled Laura out into the snow beyond the front porch. The maid was right behind him and didn't waste a second leaving the premises.

A moment later the scream came again, louder, distorted by pain and something else. It did not cease, but instead trailed off, fading in the distance though none of them were moving.

Crowley looked back at the house, a frown on his features, and studied the structure carefully.

Silence greeted him, complete and eternal. The dead that had been in the house were gone and so too the man who had summoned them to visit and paid them in blood to stay away every year.

Laura charged past him, screaming her uncle's name. He let her go, knowing full well what she would find inside.

The house was as empty as his own; devoid of family or loved ones. Once upon a time he'd lost his family too; the difference was he knew better than to try to summon them back.

The wind called out, blasting past the empty house, drowning the sounds of a woman in mourning. Her losses were bad, but could have been worse. In the end, she still had her husband and her children waiting for her.

That would have to be enough.

Crowley scratched at his left hand again and looked down, annoyed. He did not, as a rule, get itchy skin without a damned good reason. Almost nothing could kill him and even things that could failed to make the death stick.

The back of his left hand had a white patch on it.

He looked carefully and frowned.

Greasepaint. He'd dealt with that exact color only a week or so earlier. Titanium white.

Crowley pulled out his handkerchief and rubbed at the stuff. He could see it come off of his flesh and stick to the fine cotton weave.

Still, as much as he wiped the paint away, there was more of it underneath.

And as he watched, the patch grew a bit. And then it grew a bit more.

Crowley scowled.

Somewhere in hell, he suspected a dead clown was laughing.

Changing Faces

Arnie Miller's day started poorly and went downhill fast. First, there was getting out of bed and stepping on Fireball's tail. That was a bad start, indeed. Fireball was the cute little ball of fluff his girlfriend had picked up for him four years ago. Somewhere along the way, his girlfriend Suzie had run off with a man who built custom made motorcycles and the ball of fluff became a twenty-seven-pound eating machine with a bad attitude, a powerful need to cough up fur balls, and claws large enough to open eight running wounds down Arnie's leg.

As Arnie let out a yowl of his own, Fireball cut loose with a steam kettle shriek and sank fangs into the back of Arnie's knee. From there it was almost a foregone conclusion that Arnie would fall forward and crack his head on the edge of his nightstand.

Oh, yes! A good start to the day.

When he woke up for the second time, Arnie looked around and noticed that the cat had decided to let him live for another day. There was a lump on the side of his head that felt slightly smaller than an ostrich egg, and the bleeding wounds in his calf had dwindled down to mere trickles instead of actual rivers of blood.

"I hate Mondays." It was Tuesday, but he'd been given a very nasty bonk on the head so really, he should be forgiven this oversight.

Arnie made it to the bathroom and took care of his daily business. The shower was a pleasure, but shaving was always a pain. He did it anyway, because it was easier to put on the grease paint if he didn't have to hide all the stubble.

After he finished cleaning and shaving he made himself a quick breakfast of scrambled eggs and toast and watched half an hour of the news. Nothing happy going on that he could see and one of his acquaintances had been violently mutilated.

He thought about that for a second, the toast trembling in his hand. Matthew Sechrist was dead. Maddy the Clown was deceased, and not by natural causes. Maddy was a good guy, too, if a bit of a whiner. They'd sat together on several occasions at the end of this birthday party or that local fair and smoked and drank and talked about women. Mostly they talked about the fact that remarkably few women found clowns sexy and lamented that they'd never gotten better careers.

Still, he loved the kids. It was bad about Maddy. He was a good man, and Arnie would drink a few to him later, after the fair was done. For now, it was time to get ready, so he got himself off the sofa, scarfed down the last of his eggs, he put on his war paint: Titanium white face and a big blue curly-haired wig: blue triangles under his eyes and above them as well, a bright red smile and blue dimples to accent it. Finally, of course, the red nose. Next came his regalia: A loose, gigantic white outfit with green polka dots, and an orange tie with matching green spots; two Purple shoes, size 32, and a top hat that was a perfect match for his oversized tie.

The Ford Bronco was looking a little like a salvage job pulled from the river, but that was to be expected as it had, indeed, been pulled from the Miskatonic River after Bonko the Clown "borrowed" it last year. Bonko was already up for parole, and Arnie hoped there were no hard feelings. It was bad for business when the clowns started throwing down and beating the hell out of each other. Also, Bonko was a mean bastard and he fought dirty.

The Hamilton Mills Textile Company was having their annual Summer Fair this week. Walter Hamilton was a rich old bastard with a great sense of humor and a love for children. Every year he did the week-long carnival and he went all out, hiring the best rides (checked carefully for safety regulations) and damned near every clown in a three-county radius. It was a good thing, and the pay was top dollar. There were kids all over the place and a lot of them even came from the local orphanages. Really, when he thought of old Walter Hamilton, it made Arnie glad he was a clown. The old man was positively inspirational.

The drive to Hamilton Park was short and Arnie took his time. The weather was about as perfect as he could have hoped for, too. Nice and crisp, without being too cold.

The fair didn't open for at least another hour, but Arnie liked to get there early. That way he could check out all the rides, scope out the corner he was going to work, and have all his equipment set up. Arnie liked to multitask and they paid extra if you brought your own supplies. Arnie brought balloons and helium tanks. Most of the balloons would go for passing out to kids, but he also had a special selection for making animals.

He unloaded the tanks of helium and set himself up in a corner near the funnel cakes booth. Funnel cakes were what made fairs the most fun for him and Arnie could eat the damned things like there was no tomorrow.

There were already a lot of people milling around and he could see not one but two buses of kids pulling up. They were from a collection of foster homes and from the state orphanage. Unlike most of the locals they got a free pass to the rides and coupons for several snacks, courtesy of Hamilton.

"Is that you, Arnie?" He recognized Lou's voice immediately. Lou was close to three hundred pounds of happy, cheerful man who went by the name of Mister Peasely. He was one of the more subdued clowns in town; his outfit was more along the lines of a hobo, even if all of the choices in accoutrements were exaggerated.

"You'd know it was me if you'd wear your glasses, Lou." He smiled to take any risk of insult out of the comment.

Lou smiled back. "I'm wearing my contacts, smart ass. It's this damned pollen. I can't get them to stay in place so good. They keep drying out."

"Yeah? Still, I don't exactly look like I'm in street clothes." Arnie set down the last of his helium canisters and unloaded a run of strings he'd cut in advance and the plugs he'd use to seal the balloons when they were filled. Every balloon had his face on it on one side and on the other it had an ad for the textile mill and the fair. The balloons were free because of the mention of the fair, and that was a big plus, because he also passed them out for free.

"You'd think so, wouldn't you? But I saw a clown with almost the same face over near the merry-go-round." Lou said the words with a false casual voice.

"Excuse me?" There was nothing mild in Arnie's voice. Clown faces were serious business. Every clown tried to look unique. Hell, there had been lawsuits over faces that were too similar and Arnie didn't much want to get involved in one of those. His face was close to one that had been used back in the sixties. He'd seen the clown as a kid and been stuck with that face in his mind, because the guy had left such an impression on him. It wasn't like he'd stolen the design: he'd just borrowed heavily from it. Besides, he remembered hearing the clown and his whole troupe had died a few months later in a bad fire.

"I'm not trying to start any trouble, Arnie. I just figured you should know is all." The man looked away from him, his blue eyes staring across the park in the direction of the ride he'd just mentioned. Lou was a good guy, but he was also a certified gossip monger and loved causing trouble. Arnie normally took anything the man said with a grain of salt, but this? This was different.

"Well, thanks for that, Lou. I guess I better go check out the competition." He didn't want to, but now that the other clown had been mentioned, it was time to see if he and the new guy really looked that much alike and, if they did, whether or not they could come to some sort of agreeable terms.

The time flies when you're having fun. By the time Arnie found the other clown, the fair had opened. The man was dressed in a bright red coat and suit, with enough sequins to just about blind a person. Unlike a lot of the clowns, his outfit looked custom tailored to fit his tall, lean body. The outfit looked as if it had just been made and was finished off with a matching top hat and well-polished dress shoes, complete with dark red spats. He was, without a doubt, the most dapper clown Arnie had ever seen.

His back was turned to Arnie at first and he was handing out a variety of trinkets to the kids around him ranging from paper flowers to whoopee cushions, the sort of things the kids could take with them and hold on to for years if they were careful. Whoever he was, he had his act in gear and he was damned good. Arnie kept watching for a while as the clown went through his routine.

A pretty young thing went by with a Young Turk boyfriend in tow: She wasn't more than fifteen years old and had basically ignored the clown's performance as she nibbled on cotton candy. The clown bowed his head so that the top hat rolled down, caught his jacket and wheeled its way down to his gloved hand. The hand caught the brim of the hat and as the clown looked at the girl and winked, a dozen paper roses popped from within it, an offering to her looks.

The entire group of children and adults alike applauded the simple gesture. As the girl reached for the flowers, the clown tapped the brim of his hat and all but one of them receded into the depths of the topper before he flicked his wrist and sent it back the way it had come. With disgusting efficiency, he spun his body just a bit caught the remaining flower as it fell from the hat, and bowed from the waist as he handed it to the absolutely stunned young girl. Even her boyfriend, who had started to look just a mite jealous, applauded and smiled.

And Arnie looked at the face for the first time as the clown did his stunts. The hair was dark blue, several shades darker than Arnie's wig, and it looked to be real. It was just as curly but longer. It was the face that made Arnie's heart sink down into his stomach and dance a nervous Watusi. Two triangles started at the edge of the eyebrows and rose toward the hair above. Below the eyes, two more dark blue triangles dropped down and pointed toward the smiling red lips; a small red dot was painted at the very tip of his nose and colored the dimples that he'd painted over the proper spots on his face.

He wasn't exactly like Arnie, but the similarities were very, very strong. Maybe even lawsuit strong.

The clown looked at him and Arnie saw shock on the thin face, written under the makeup that left a smile painted in place.

"Well, what have we here, boys and girls?" Arnie blinked as the clown spun toward him, the bright blue eyes looking him over from top to bottom.

"Is that your brother, Rufo?" The voice came from a swarthy little cherub with big brown eyes. Christ, even the little kids could see the similarities.

"Why yes!" The clown, Rufo, apparently, positively beamed as he looked over his shoulder and patted the toddler on the cheek before producing a silver dollar that looked like it had been minted before the Korean War and handing it to the kid. Through all those gestures, his eyes never left Arnie's. "Yes, indeed! It's my long-lost brother! This is a good reason for a celebration, wouldn't you say?"

Arnie swallowed hard and tried to recover from the unexpected change. The lanky clown moved over to him and slid up beside him with slick, almost spidery motions.

He leaned in close, and put his lips next to Arnie's ear. "What's your name, Ace?"

"F-Fast Freddie."

Rufo sprang back as soon as Arnie had answered. "Fast Freddie! I thought I'd never see you again!" His voice went up in octaves, high enough to almost sound feminine, and then he jumped forward and wrapped his arms around Arnie in a wild, exaggerated hug. Before Arnie knew what was happening, he was off the ground, lifted like he was little more than a child by the man who was thinner than he was.

The arms around his ribcage squeezed like a python and for a moment he thought his ribs would break. Then he was set down and Rufo stepped back, grinning broadly for everyone.

"A family reunion! Let's all have ice cream!" He capered around for a few moments and pointed his gloved hand at the ice cream stand a dozen feet away. Most of the kids looked, distracted by the idea of a treat.

Arnie was following the man's every move, so he didn't really understand how the other clown had just vanished, but that was exactly what happened. He looked away for only an instant and Rufo was gone.

It felt like butterflies were eating away the lining of his stomach, and the vicious bastards were hungry.

They were eating their way through him solely because of the vibe he got off the other clown. There was a serious feeling that something was not right with Rufo the clown and that sense was only increased by the strength of the man. Arnie touched his ribs where the man had held him, feeling a dull ache from the force of the grip.

He looked around and shook his head. He'd wanted to handle the makeup thing as easily and painlessly as possible. Maybe Rufo wanted that too, but he wouldn't know until they ran across each other again. The fair was large, but not gigantic. They'd see each other.

Arnie wasn't comforted by that thought.

A little past noon, when the initial rush of children had become a large tide of people, Arnie spotted the other clown again. He was taking a break, leaning against the funnel cake stand and scarfing down a fried and powdered sugar-coated confection, when he heard someone whimpering.

"Please…Please mister, I did like you asked, didn't I?" Arnie tried to swallow his mouthful of funnel cake and choked on it a bit when he recognized Lou's voice.

The sounds were coming from one booth over, where the ring-toss stand was, and Arnie looked around the rear corner of his resting spot and saw Lou trembling.

"You sure did, Mister Peasley. You did it just as nice and right as you could have, and that's why I gave you the fifty bucks." The voice was low and raspy and sent shivers of gooseflesh across Arnie's back.

"Then why are you doing this?" Lou's voice cracked a bit. "I swear I won't tell no one, honest injun."

All around him Arnie could hear the sounds of the fair in full swing. There were children laughing and screaming excitedly and the rattle and clank of a dozen different rides in motion. Tinny music came out of cheap speakers at a dozen different stands and he knew that if he looked back toward the front of the funnel cake stand, he'd see easily fifty people milling around and having a good time.

"Know what the problem with you is, Mister Peasely?"

Lou shook his head.

"The problem is you sold out one of your friends for fifty bucks. How trustworthy do you think that makes you?"

Arnie held his breath, looking for the source of the voice he heard. He had a feeling he knew who it was, but he had to make one hundred percent sure. All he could see was the shadow that fall across Lou's pudgy, aging body.

"Oh God, Oh God, please no…" Lou backed up, his head shaking from side to side, and as he moved back the source of the shadow stepped forward. Rufo the clown looked at Mister Peasely and grinned.

"That's just what Maddy said, right before I ripped his eyes out."

Ever see a clown run in fear? It isn't pretty. Lou tried to spin on his heels and beat a retreat, but the landscape of the park tricked him. His oversized shoes caught themselves on one of the many small shrubs around the edge of the park and he went down fast and hard. His face slammed into the ground and he rolled over, gasping for breath and trying to see past the clod of dirt his makeup managed to attract.

Rufo moved forward with unnerving grace. He didn't hurry and he didn't worry about tripping over any of the litter that had already accumulated in the areas behind the concession stands and carnie games.

"What's that, Mister Peasely?" The man leaned over Lou and scrutinized his face.

"What's what?" Lou gasped as he started to sit up.

Rufo's hand shot forward and grabbed at Lou's face. Arnie watched on, unbelieving, as the clown rammed his gloved thumb into the soft orb of Lou's left eye. "You've got something in your eye..."

Lou let out a shriek and bucked as the clown kept pushing. Arnie coughed hard, and almost choked on the forgotten confection in his mouth.

Rufo laughed, a sound that had nothing whatsoever to do with joy.

Then Rufo did it again. He reached out with free hand and caught Lou's tongue between his finger and thumb. Lou kept screaming, trying to get away as the red flowed from his closed eyelid.

Rufo pulled back and Lou's head followed for a moment before the flesh of his tongue sliced away from his mouth.

"Jesus Christ!" Arnie opened his mouth and said the words before he realized what he was doing. He froze for a moment, his hands slapping against his mouth as if to block any more foolish utterances.

"Oh, Fast Freddie, I don't think He's here right now, do you?" Rufo winked at him and dropped Lou's tongue to the ground.

"I-Unnn." Nothing good was working past his hands, but his damned mouth kept trying to make a proper sound, something along the lines of a plea for mercy, he suspected.

"Got better things to do with His time than mess with a few clowns working out their differences." Rufo stepped closer. "And that's all this us, right? A few clowns working things out." Rufo stopped coming forward and the sneer under his blood red smile grew broader, baring perfectly even, perfectly white teeth. "By the way, Arnie, did I ever say you could steal my face?"

Arnie felt his bladder threaten a revolution and shook his head violently.

"I wanted to talk to you about that," he squeaked.

Rufo came closer, flicking his fingertips to remove the pesky blood that insisted on staining his gloves. "Well, now seems like a good time to me." He looked around and saw Lou curled up in a fetal position behind him, blood dribbling from his mouth and spilling across the dirt and grass. "I have a few minutes to spare."

"I just want to talk, okay? I can change my makeup. I will. No problem."

Rufo looked at him again, his light blue eyes all a twinkle. "Yeah? Pretty sure you can use Peasely's. He won't need it anymore."

Arnie shook his head. He wanted to have a nice, rational conversation, but every time he thought he'd be able to open his mouth and talk, his tongue got all knotted up. *Hey, not like Lou's! Lou's is just fine, sitting over there on the ground. Is that an ant on his tongue? I think it is. Isn't it cats that are supposed to get tongues?*

Arnie cackled instead of speaking. He kept looking at the fat black ant chewing at Lou's tongue and it kept looking funnier and funnier. "Ant got your tongue, Lou? Heh-heh-heh." He fell back and slapped his knees as he guffawed. It wasn't funny! He kept trying to tell himself that, but it wasn't working. He was so fucking nervous that everything seemed funny in comparison to facing the psychopath in front of him.

Rufo moved toward him like a speeding train and grabbed at his hair, knocking his top hat aside. The other clown seemed positively shocked when the blue curly wig came off in his hand, and Arnie saw the look on the man's painted face and fell on his ass laughing.

Oh God his stomach hurt from laughing so hard and he was having trouble catching his breath. And Rufo looked at him, shaking his head and actually grinning a bit himself.

"You get points for that, Arnie. That was genuinely funny."

Rufo sat down in the grass and shoved the wig inside the top hat.

Eventually, Arnie calmed down, and started catching his breath.

"Okay, Arnie. What we have here is a problem."

"You gonna kill me?" Arnie had no doubt the clown could. None at all. There was something about the man under that paint that unsettled him. Probably it was the violent tendencies.

Rufo looked his way and shrugged. "Well, I should. I mean, look at what I did to Mister Peasely over there, and he really didn't do that much to offend me."

"Why did you do it?"

"Why?" Rufo looked back at Lou, who was starting to crawl around. "Well, he really wasn't a very good clown, was he? I didn't see him make a single kid laugh."

Arnie stared at the clown for several seconds. "But you just got here today..."

"I wasn't wearing my face yesterday." He shrugged his shoulders almost casually and as if to dismiss the entire sordid affair, but the grin on his face belied that attitude. "Without the makeup we're all just faces in the crowd. Why do you think clowns protect their faces so avidly?"

"So, are you going to kill me?" Arnie heard the quaver in his voice but could do nothing to stop it.

Rufo turned again, distracted by the sound of Lou finally managing to stand up. Lou's Mister Peasely Makeup was all a mess, covered with dirt, grass and blood like it was. The chunky clown staggered to the left and knocked over a trash can with a loud clatter.

Rufo turned back to him with a thin smile hidden under his bright red lips. "Here's a deal for you. Go finish my light work," he pointed over his shoulder to indicate Lou, "and I'll let you live just as long as you change your makeup."

"What?'

Rufo's eyes rolled toward the heavens. "I said, go kill Peasely and I'll let you live. You have to change the makeup, but other than that, we'll be even-stevens."

"You can't be serious."

Rufo popped up to a standing position like a Jack-in-the-box and moved toward Arnie. Arnie flinched back as the other clown got right in his face. "Is this the face of a joker? Of course I'm serious! You or Peasely, who do you value more in this world?" Rufo stepped away from him and bowed at the waist, sweeping his right arm in Lou's direction. Lou was standing again, but weaving like a boxer who'd taken a nasty beating. His bloodied eye was swollen shut and the color of his skin under his makeup was almost as pasty white as Arnie's clown face.

"I can't kill Lou. He's my friend?"

"He sold you out for fifty dollars, Fast Freddie. He took chump change to let me know you were wearing my face. Now what does that tell you?" Rufo stayed back, looking at Arnie with eyes that almost seemed to glitter.

"It's no never mind to me, sport. I just figured I'd give an option that guaranteed your safety. Something to let you sleep better at night."

Arnie swallowed hard and looked at Lou. "But, he was just letting you know, right? I mean, that's a common decency thing."

"Hardly." Rufo stepped back against the concession stand wall and looked around, as if making sure there would be no witnesses. "What he should have done, if he was going to be decent about things, is he should have just told me and everything could have been worked out without any real troubles. Instead, he asked for money. Not very sporting of him, now was it?"

"But…I already said I'd switch my face. I can even let you decide what it should look like." He wanted time, a way out of the situation, but it wasn't going so well.

"I never said I was going to kill you, Fast Freddie. You just made an assumption." Rufo closed his eyes, looking remarkably bored with the conversation. "You don't have to buy your way out of things. You can just take your chances."

"You killed one man and maimed another." The man was insane. That was all there was to it. Sooner or later he'd slip up and let someone live. That someone would be Arnie, provided he committed cold blooded murder. He just couldn't do it. Not to Lou, not to anyone. Arnie wasn't a violent man.

"I never said your chances would be good."

"I can't do this. I'm not a killer." He shook his head and looked at the ground between his feet.

"Not even if it was a mercy killing?"

Arnie couldn't think of a proper response. So he went with the first thing that came to mind. "Okay, you took his tongue, but there's always a life as a mime."

"Now how is living as a *mime* a good thing?" The other clown sounded indignant.

"Well…Okay. That's true." He wasn't doing his best job of winning the argument.

Rufo pushed off the wall and took fast strides to reach Lou, who by that point was paler than ever and starting to look just plain putrid. Lou's eyes flew wide as the clown approached him and he shook his head violently.

Rufo grabbed Lou by the back of his neck pushed him toward Arnie. He didn't let go, and for all the world it looked like he was lifting Lou off the ground.

"Mnuaaahhh!" Lou was trying to say something, but the lack of tongue was slowing down comprehension.

"Now you hush, Mister Peasely. The grownups are talking." Rufo threw Lou to the ground and the man bounced on his knees with an audible cracking noise. He let out a grunt and fell face forward into the turf. Without any hesitation, Rufo cocked back his leg and punted across the older clown's wide posterior, sending in forward by a good seven inches.

Lou was crying into the grass, his face bloodied and tear-streaked, while Arnie looked at him, horrified.

"Couldn't we just settle it all in court?" Arnie's voice was failing him and he squeaked like kid whose voice was just starting to break.

"Freddie," Rufo bent forward, his hands resting on his knees. "If I wanted to go to court, I'd have to prove to everyone that I'm still alive. You aren't worth the effort." He stood back up and looked down on Lou and Arnie alike. "Besides, there's that whole murder and mutilation thing to consider. Most courts don't like it when clowns go all violent."

"So you just want me to..."

"Kill him. Go ahead. I can even give instructions if it'll help."

Arnie was having trouble catching his breath. He kept sucking in but the air didn't seem to get where it needed to go.

"Don't have all day here, you know. There are kids to entertain." His voice was as cold as a February morning.

"I can't do it." Arnie felt the tears when they started, and shook his head. "I can't. I'm not a murderer."

"Just a thief."

"I didn't know I was copying your makeup, okay? I didn't know it wasn't original!" He screamed now, his voice carrying down the narrow alley of concession stands.

Rufo reared back and then stepped forward, his foot landing on Lou's wrist. Bones snapped and the older man let out a blubbering squeal of pain. "Liar!"

Arnie trembled, his breaths becoming nothing more than eager gasps.

"No. I'm not."

"I remember you!" Rufo's eyes narrowed down to angry slits, the blue of his makeup replacing the blue of his eyes. "I saw you when you were a little boy, with your mother and father, when you were in Long Island. I saw you in the crowd, you lying bastard. I gave you a chocolate coin and you ate it." He ground his foot down and Lou made another cry, this one much weaker. "I saw you take the one from your little sister, too. She never said a thing, just watched you eat it."

Guilt washed over Arnie. Not because of his sister's chocolate, because she'd certainly stolen enough of his things in the past, but because the man looking at him was right. He'd known full well where the makeup he wore came from.

"But, I heard you died. Heard the whole carnival went under in a fire of some kind."

"There's dead and then there's dead. I'm here now and I have to say, I don't much like thieves, Arnie."

He flinched at the use of his real name.

"How did you know?"

"I never forget a face. And I always keep my word. So here are your choices, Arnie. One last time. You can kill your fat friend here," he paused long enough to grind the ruin of Lou's wrist again. "Or you can take your chances that I'm a forgiving clown."

Arnie took option number three and pushed off the ground, standing up. He didn't let himself think about it, he just took a swing; his fist connected with Rufo's jaw and sent the other clown staggering backward. The impact sent a jolt through his hand and wrist.

"Oh my..." Rufo purred as he looked at Arnie. "Got a pair hiding somewhere in there after all, don't you?"

"I don't want to fight you and I won't kill Lou." His knees were shaking with adrenaline, but he didn't back down. "You just go away. I'll change my makeup. I'll even quit being a clown if that's what you want. But you just go away."

Rufo stared at him for several seconds, the grin under his smile unwavering. Then he stepped forward and drove the heel of his foot into the flabby neck of Lou, who was still lying on the ground and moaning. Lou's face shoved hard into the dirt, and Arnie heard the bones in his neck breaking. There was no mistaking the sound, or the fact that it killed Lou instantly.

"I'm here to stay, Fast Freddie."

Arnie screamed. That was a bit more than he was willing to deal with, and he let loose with a girly shriek and bolted past the funnel cake stand and into the main area of the fair. People all through the open field turned and looked at him as he ran, following his actions with their eyes and in some cases even pointing to him as if he were part of the entertainment.

He stopped when he'd cleared a good fifty yards and looked back, fully expecting Rufo to be on his heels, but there was nothing, no one.

The rent-a-cop showed up a minute later to check on him. He was tall, skinny and looked like a good breeze would send him blowing away like a paper doll.

"What happened?"

Arnie looked at the security guard, looked back from where he'd run, and shook his head. The guard regarded him with suspicion and then moved in the direction of the funnel cake stand.

"I wouldn't go there if I were you." The words came out as a whisper.

Arnie moved toward his truck, wanting more than anything else to forget everything that was happening around him. Enough was too much in this case. It was time to get a drink or even just to get out of town before the freak with the same clown face came after him a second time.

He tried not to think about the fact that the man had accused him of stealing candy from his little sister. Every time he thought about that little fact, he got that giggly feeling in his stomach and wanted to break into hysterical laughter again. It wasn't a bad feeling, but it didn't really help his current situation.

He could come back later, he reasoned, with a real policeman. The truck started just like it was supposed to and he looked into the rearview mirror before backing up. So no one could have been more surprised than he was when the rear tire lifted over a bump and came down with an audible crunching sound.

Arnie jammed his foot down on the brake pedal and waited a few seconds with a sickening feeling growing in his stomach. He was just about to open the door and look behind the truck when the screaming started.

Four elderly women were looking at the truck with horrified expressions painted on their faces, and Arnie knew before he finally gathered the courage to peek. The tilt of the truck should have been his first signal. But he knew Lou well enough, knew the shoes he saw stretched out on the asphalt beyond the end of his truck, too. Mister Peasely's body rested under the left rear tire, his head already pulped beyond repair by the weight of the vehicle.

Arnie climbed out of the truck with a whistling wheezing sound coming from his lungs. He shook his head violently to get rid of the tears that were starting to blur his vision. Sadly, the truck was still in gear and continued its trek over Lou's backside, crushing more of the corpse as it moved. When it was done with Mister Peasely it ran back into the rear bumper of a soccer sticker-covered SUV and set off the car alarm.

"Oh he screwed me. I'm so fucked..."

The rent-a-cop showed up around that time and moved straight for Arnie, his face set in lines of disgust. The skinny man moved fast and tackled him, though Arnie didn't try to defend himself. He was still too focused on what was left of Lou.

By the time the police arrived, the security guard had Arnie hog tied with plastic bags and was strutting around like a rooster. The cops untied Arnie long enough to ask him a few hundred questions. When they were finished, Arnie was in the back of a police cruiser and wearing actual handcuffs instead of plastic bags.

It took three days for Arnie to get up the bail to get out of his jail cell. During that time he was subjected to several sexual advances and had both of his oversized shoes stolen from the possessions locker.

He didn't much mind. One way or the other, his career as a clown was at an end.

The newspapers and news programs had a field day with the death of Mister Peasely. Within seventy-two hours of the incident, Arnie's face was known far and wide across the area. Both his clown face and the one he wore under it. Speculations ran far and wide about whether he was responsible for the murders of several clowns that had occurred in the last couple of years, but most of them had dwindled down to a trickle when the fact that he'd never left the state came out. Most of the deaths had taken place in upper state New York.

His answering machine was full of messages ranging from requests for interviews to death threats from several of his colleagues and one small child who claimed a mime had killed his best friend. He listened to all of them as he fended off another assault from Fireball, who was a little pissy after three days without food.

Arnie got a cold Budweiser out of his refrigerator after he'd taken care of feeding the resident predatory feline. He sat down and pulled the tab and sighed mightily to himself.

It was possible that he could work this to his advantage, but he wasn't sure just how. There were a dozen manuscripts for children's books sitting in his desk drawers. He supposed that was a possibility.

"I just wanted to make the kids happy, really. I like kids." He knocked back half of his beer in salute the children and let out a deeply satisfying belch.

"That's why I've decided to let you live anyway." Rufo's voice came from directly behind him.

Arnie couldn't have jumped any higher if someone had electrified his ass. The other clown was standing behind Arnie's recliner, smiling, with Fireball in his hands. The traitorous cat was slumped along the clown's forearm and purring.

"I thought about it, Arnie. You're a good clown. You make kids laugh." He shrugged and let Fireball drop into the chair, where the beast promptly got comfortable again.

Arnie looked carefully at the clown in front of him and shivered. The face he wore wasn't makeup. The triangles of blue had been cut into the other clown's face; as had the red lips and the dimples and the dot on his nose. He'd been wearing makeup to hide that fact at the fair.

"See why I'm partial to my looks, Arnie? They aren't going to go away. Find a new face and we'll get along just fine."

"They're going to convict me for murdering Lou."

"Best they have on you is a tragic accident and you panicking. It's all just hype, the rest of it. All just smoke and mirrors." He smiled brightly. "We know all about that sort of thing, don't we, Fast Freddie?"

Arnie just looked at the man and shivered. Insanity seemed to come off of Rufo in a palpable wave.

"I'm done here. Change your face, or the next time I see you, I'll cut your face off your skull and make it into a seat cushion. Do we understand each other?"

Arnie nodded his head so hard he thought he might break his own neck from the force.

"Take care of Fireball. He'll be watching you. Oh, I read your manuscripts and made a few suggestions. Good luck with that."

The clown headed for the front door and stopped with his hand on the knob. "You know if you mention me they'll think you're crazy, right?"

"I won't mention you."

"Good. You'd be miserable if you had to go through all that therapy." He sniffed the air. "Take a shower, you stink."

"Been in lock up," Arnie explained apologetically.

"Yeah. Bonko's getting out tomorrow. He's probably gonna want to talk to you about the three years for stealing your truck."

Arnie nodded his head and smiled. "He's a bad clown."

"What do we do with bad clowns, Arnie?"

That was a quandary. He really wasn't sure how to answer, but the longer he looked in Rufo's eyes, the more he thought he understood. "We-we punish them?"

Rufo nodded and smiled. "That we do, Arnie. Take care of my light work for me, okay?"

Bonko was a big boy and he fought dirty, but Arnie nodded anyway. "I think I can do that. I really think I can."

Rufo nodded one last time and quietly slipped through the door.

Arnie moved to the kitchen and looked at his assortment of knives. There were a couple of them that would fit through Bonko's ribs without any trouble at all, and the meat cleaver, well that could do a lot of damage to Bonko's head.

"Gonna need a new face, anyway. Bonko's was always nice."

About the Author

JAMES A. MOORE authored more than forty novels. The first decades of his career focused on his love for horror, as seen in many novels including the critically acclaimed *Fireworks, Under the Overtree, Blood Red,* and the Serenity Falls trilogy. Later, Jim earned a reputation as the "prince of grimdark fantasy" with his hugely popular Seven Forges series as well as the Tides of War trilogy. The author loved collaborating with other writers, most frequently with Christopher Golden on the Bloodstained Worlds trilogy and with Charles R. Rutledge on the Griffin & Price series, among others. Nominated for the Bram Stoker Award twice, Moore won the Shirley Jackson Award for co-editing *The Twisted Book of Shadows*. He first came to prominence as one of the principal world-builders involved in the World of Darkness from White Wolf Games, most famously Vampire: The Masquerade and Werewolf: The Apocalypse. At the time of his passing, Moore left behind one completed solo fantasy novel, as well as completed collaborations with Charles R. Rutledge and Mary SanGiovanni. Plans are afoot to bring those to readers soon.

Bibliography

NOVELS

The Black Stone Bay Series
Blood Red (with "Blood Tide"
Blood Harvest
Bloodlines

The Bloodstained Series (w/Christopher Golden)
Bloodstained Oz
Bloodstained Wonderland
Bloodstained Neverland

The Chris Corin Series

Possessions

Newbies

Rabid Growth

The Chronicles of Jonathan Crowley

Under the Overtree

Writ in Blood: Serenity Falls, Book One

The Pack: Serenity Falls, Book Two

Dark Carnival: Serenity Falls, Book Three

Cherry Hill

Smile No More

Boomtown

One Bad Week

Where the Sun Goes to Die

The Griffin & Price Series (w/Charles Rutledge)

Blind Shadows

Congregations of the Dead

A Hell Within

The Seven Forges Series

Seven Forges

The Blasted Lands

City of Wonders

The Silent Army

The Godless

The War Born

The Subject Seven Series

Subject Seven

Run

The Tides of War Series

The Last Sacrifice

Fallen Gods

Gates of the Dead

Standalone Novels

Deeper

Fireworks

Harvest Moon

The Haunted Forest Tour (w/ Jeff Strand)

NOVELLAS

Dear Diary: Run Like Hell

Homestead

The Wild Hunt

SHORT STORY COLLECTIONS

Slices

This is Halloween

CROSSROAD
PRESS

www.ingramcontent.com/pod-product-compliance
Lightning Source LLC
Chambersburg PA
CBHW020636180626
46816CB00003B/997

* 9 7 8 1 6 3 7 8 9 2 9 8 5 *